NO QUARTER FOR A RUSTLER

The rustler rode out of the corral with a rifle in his hand, waving a white cloth tied to the end of it. He moved toward Dundee.

Dundee recognized Jason Karnes and noticed how the man's leg was held out stiffly away from the saddle. *A little souvenir I gave him.* They stared cold-eyed at each other a minute before Dundee said, "I bet that was *you* who shot at me a little while ago."

Karnes nodded. "It was."

"I'm pleased to find your aim ain't improved much."

"It'll get better. I got me a crippled leg now. They say when a man loses one thing, he gains someplace else. I'm counting on a better shooting eye."

"You ought to've counted on your horse-picking eye and cut you out a fast one to get you away from here. Old Man Titus is up yonder on that hill, hideburner, and he's come to see blood."

LLANO RIVER

ELMER KELTON

BANTAM BOOKS
TORONTO · NEW YORK · LONDON · SYDNEY · AUCKLAND

LLANO RIVER

A Bantam Book / February 1982
2nd printing . . . April 1988

ISBN 0-553-27119-9

Published simultaneously in the United States and Canada

Bantam Books are published by Bantam Books, a division of Bantam
Doubleday Dell Publishing Group, Inc. Its trademark, consisting of the
words ''Bantam Books'' and the portrayal of a rooster, is Registered in
U.S. Patent and Trademark Office and in other countries. Marca
Registrada. Bantam Books, 666 Fifth Avenue, New York, New York
10103.

PRINTED IN THE UNITED STATES OF AMERICA

KR   11 10 9 8 7 6 5 4 3 2

I

Some men seem blessed with a jovial nature, an even humor that lets them take reversal and insult in stride without losing their smile or clenching a fist.

Dundee was not one of these. His temper was like a hammer cocked back over forty grains of black powder. The echo racketed for miles when Old Man Farraday brought a new son-in-law out to the ranch and handed him Dundee's job as foreman. A man with any self-respect couldn't just stand there like a sheep and abjectly accept demotion to cowhand thataway. So after the discussion was over, Dundee painfully rubbed his bruised knuckles and asked for his time.

He had stopped in a ragtag shipping-pen settlement later to wash away the indignities and suffered one more: he lost most of his payoff money over a whisky-splashed card table.

He had no clear idea where he was riding to. In the Texas free-range days of the '80s, a man seeking fresh grass usually drifted in a westerly direction. He might veer a little northward, or southward, but the main direction was always west, for that was where the "new" was, where a man could cut a fresh deck and hope for a new deal all around. Dundee had ridden several days. Now darkness was about to catch him as his half-Thoroughbred bay splashed across a narrow creek toward a dusty little cowtown which the sign said was Titusville. His outlook hadn't improved much as the bay had slowly put the long miles behind him. Dundee was tired, hungry, near broke, and ringy enough to do bare-handed battle with a bobcat.

The two-rut wagon road widened into a many-rutted street. At the head of it Dundee passed a set of horse corrals and a big barn that said "Titus Livery." He thought how much the bay would like a clean stall and a good bait of oats. A little way down the hoof-softened street he saw a thin little man lighting a lantern on the front gallery of a long frame building. The sign by the front door said "Titus Hotel." Dundee looked with appreciation at the deep, narrow windows and imagined how soft the mattresses were, how pleasant must be the bright colors of the wallpaper. But he jingled the few coins left in his pockets and knew that after a drink and a meal, he'd retrace his steps down to the creekbank, stake the bay on grass and stretch his own frame on a blanket, looking up at stars instead of wallpaper.

Slim pickings, sure enough, but there wasn't any use a man biting himself like a stirred-up rattler. If he was strong he took the hand which was dealt him and played it through, even when it was all jokers. Tomorrow he'd scout around and try to find him a ranch job. Tonight, the hell with it.

He saw the words "Titus Mercantile" on a big, false-fronted building, and "Titus Saloon" on still another. *Ain't there nobody here but Titus?* he asked himself irritably.

Across the street lay a narrow, deep building which he took to be a second saloon, and he angled the bay toward it. On the porch, a lanky man sat rocked back in a rawhide chair, balanced against the clapboard wall. The sign over his head read: "Texas Bar." Since it didn't say anything about Titus, Dundee decided to give the place a try. *That Titus is already rich enough,* he thought. *No use giving him my business.* He stepped off of the horse and dropped the reins through a ring in a cedar post, taking a hitch to be sure the bay didn't get a fool notion to wander off in search of Titus, whoever the Samhill that was.

Dundee stretched himself. He dusted his felt hat across his leg, raising a small cloud. He glanced at the stubbled oldtimer in the chair and found the man sitting motionless, watching him. The man finally spoke: "Evenin'." Saloon bum, Dundee judged him by his look, by the dusty, threadbare clothes he wore, the runover old boots. If he was figuring on Dundee buying him a drink, he was out of luck. But it didn't cost anything to be civil. "Evenin'."

The tail of his eye caught a movement, and he turned. From around the side of the building three young men came ambling along as if they had all night to do whatever it might be that they had in mind. Cowboys, Dundee figured. Boil them all down and you wouldn't have fifty cents worth of tallow, or anything else. They paused at the edge of the low porch and eyed Dundee like they were appraising a bronc at a first-Monday horse sale. One of them looked at the bay, finally, and foolishly asked, "That your horse, friend?"

Dundee's voice was sharply impatient. "I ain't had a friend since a year ago last March. And you just try riding him off. You'll find out right quick whose horse he is."

His voice was rougher than he meant it to be. Damn Old Man Farraday and his flat-chested daughter and his ignorant new son-in-law, anyway! He saw a flash of anger in the young man's eyes. *I'm too touchy,* he thought. *I cut him off a little quick. But when a man asks a foolish question, he ought to expect an answer in kind.*

He went into the saloon and leaned his elbows heavily on the dark-stained bar. "A drink," he said. He glanced at his own scowling face in the cracked mirror behind the bar and quickly looked away, for he didn't like what he saw. Even as a baby, he hadn't been called pretty by anybody but his mother, and thirty years hadn't improved the situation. Right now he looked forty, face dusty and bewhiskered, brown eyes hostile, when deep down he knew he didn't have anybody to be mad at, really, except Old Man Farraday, who was a long way behind him.

The heavy-jowled bartender studied him as if trying to decide whether Dundee could pay. "Good whisky or cheap whisky?"

"It better not cost much. I'm almost as broke as I look."

The bartender's heavy moustache tugged with the beginnings of a grin. "That don't leave a man but little choice." He brought up a plain bottle from beneath the bar. "The quality ain't much, but it sure does carry authority."

Dundee choked on the first swallow and cut a hard glance at the bartender. But he couldn't say he'd been lied to. He poured himself a second glass and lifted it. "Here's to truth."

"I *told* you the truth."

"That is purely a fact."

He heard a commotion outside, and a stirring of hoofs. It struck him that that crazy cowboy just might be taking him up on his dare. In three long strides he reached the door and stopped. One cowboy was holding the bay's reins up close to the bit, trying to make the horse stand still. Behind, a second cowboy had hold of the bay's tail, stretching it taut. The third—the one who had asked the question—was using a pocketknife in an attempt to bob the tail off short.

Roaring, Dundee left the porch like a firebrand flung in fury. He barreled into the man who was holding the horse's tail and sent him staggering. The cowboy with the knife stared in disbelief at the speed of Dundee's fist streaking toward his eyes. The cowboy reeled backward and fell in the dust, a believer.

The third man turned loose of the reins and trudged forward, his fists up in a bare-knuckle boxer stance. Dundee didn't know the rules. He just went under and caught him in the belly. The cowboy buckled, gasping for breath. He went to his knees, out of the fight.

The first cowboy charged back into the fray. Dundee turned to meet him, his fists doubled hard as a sledge. Of a sudden this wasn't just any cowboy; he was Old Man Farraday, young enough to hit. Dundee thought the man got in a lick or two, but he didn't feel them. In a moment the cowboy was on the ground, out of it.

Only the pocketknife man was left. His nose was bleeding, his eyes wild, and somehow he looked a little like Old Man Farraday's son-in-law. Dundee gathered the pent-up anger of many days and delivered it into the cowboy's ribs. It was a considerable load. The cowboy cried out in pain, but he didn't stop coming. He swung fists awkwardly, trying for any kind of contact he could make. Dundee fetched him a hard lick on the chin, and another in the belly. They hurt; he could tell. But the cowboy stayed. He got his arms around Dundee and wrestled until Dundee lost his footing. Falling, he managed to twist so that the cowboy didn't land on top of him. The instant he hit the dirt he was pushing himself up again. He dropped the cowboy onto his back and straddled him, grabbing at the swinging fists.

"Boy," he gritted, "you better give up. I got you by the short hair."

Raging, the cowboy continued his struggle. Somehow now he didn't look quite so much like Farraday's son-in-law, who hadn't fought this hard. But Dundee thought of the pocketknife and the bay horse's tail, and his conscience didn't twinge as he swung at the jutting jaw. The cowboy stiffened, then went to struggling again. He was game, anyway.

"Boy," Dundee warned, "I tell you, I'm fixing to get out of sorts with you."

The struggling went on, so Dundee fetched him another lick.

The nondescript old man on the porch slowly let his chair away from the wall and pushed himself to his feet. He looked down calmly at the cowboy pinned to the ground. "Son Titus, I believe you've caused this stranger trouble enough. You better let him go."

The cowboy twisted and fought beneath Dundee's weight.

The man on the porch said a little firmer, "Son Titus, you get up and leave that stranger alone."

The cowboy relaxed. "All right, Pa. But I could've whipped him."

The older man snorted. "The day we have six inches of snow here in July, maybe you can whip him. Git up from there and dust yourself off."

Dundee pushed away from the cowboy but kept his fists clenched. That crazy button might decide to try just one more spin of the wheel. Dundee's knuckles were bruised, his breath short. He couldn't rightly remember when he'd had so satisfying a little fight.

The young cowboy's face was red-smeared. From his eyes, Dundee judged he hadn't had quite enough yet. But the older man's voice was strong with authority. "Son Titus, go wash yourself."

Son Titus turned away, looking back over his shoulder at Dundee. The look spoke of things unfinished, and things to come.

The other two cowboys got shakily to their feet, but they didn't seem much inclined to continue what they had started. *Some people,* Dundee thought, *just can't stay interested in one thing very long at a time.*

He turned back to check his horse. Wonder the bay hadn't jerked loose and run off, all that scuffling going on around him. Dundee patted the horse reassuringly. He took hold of the tail, stretching it out to see how much damage the cowboy had done, while at the same time he warily watched the bay's hind feet. It would be just like a horse to kick now that the trouble was over.

He couldn't see they had cut much hair. Dull boy, dull knife.

The man on the porch said, "Stranger, I apologize for my boy. He was just by way of having a little fun."

"It wasn't very funny to my horse."

"Little town like this, there ain't much for a young man to do to entertain himself. So it's natural they turn their hand to mischief when they see a stranger. Hope they didn't spoil the looks of your horse."

"They didn't, but it's no thanks to you. You sat right there and let them do it."

"I was curious to see if I'd judged you right."

"Well, did you?"

"Sized you up when you first come. You did just about what I expected you would. A little quicker, even. Nice job you done on them three buttons."

"If one of them was your son, you take it awful calm."

The man shrugged. "Does a boy good to get himself whipped once in a while. Teaches him humility. Come on back in. I'll stand you to a drink."

The heavy-jawed barkeep with the smiling moustache

reached beneath the bar and came up with a bottle that even *looked* better than the one Dundee had tried. He poured two glasses.

The man from the porch said, "I didn't hear your name."

"No, I don't reckon you did."

"It's none of my business, but I got to call you something."

"Dundee will do. I answer to that."

"I doubt that you answer to anybody. I'm John Titus."

Dundee nodded. "I gathered that when the boy called you Pa. You the Titus that owns everything in town?"

"Most of it. Whichaway did you ride in from?"

"Northeast."

"You been on my ranch the last twenty. . . twenty-five miles."

"You don't look like a big rancher."

"Meaning my clothes?" Titus shook his head. "Hell, everybody here knows me. I don't have to impress anybody."

"You dress up different when you go away from home?"

Titus shook his head again. "Why should I? Nobody would know me anyhow."

Dundee mulled that a while and finished his drink. He glanced at the big barkeep and back at Titus. "This saloon ain't got your name on it. How come you're in here buying whisky from the competition?"

"It's better than the kind *I* sell. Anyhow, the people who work in *my* saloon wear the knees out of their britches trying to please me. I get tired of being 'Mistered' all over the place. Badger here, he's so independent that even his mother hates him. I like a man who's a little contrary. Shows he's got character." His eyes narrowed. "*You're* a contrary man, Dundee."

Dundee didn't reply, for this was no news to him. He'd been only about fourteen when his brothers had decided they couldn't stand him anymore. They had ganged up and run him off from home.

Titus picked up the bottle and his glass and carried them

to a small round table. Dundee followed suit. Titus said, "You look tired. I hope you're figuring on spending the night in my *ho*tel."

"I expect I'll sleep out on the creekbank."

Titus gazed at him intently. "That's what I thought. Broke, ain't you?"

"What gives you that kind of a notion?"

"The look of you. It's all over you, like dark skin on a Comanche. Anyway, you're a cowboy. Cowboys are stone broke nine-tenths of the time."

"I won't go hungry."

"You don't have to. You need a job, I need a man. I bet we could work up a deal." Titus passed. "I seen a carbine on your saddle. You know how to use it, I expect."

"I generally hit what I aim at."

"How about a pistol?"

"Got one in my saddlebag. Always liked a carbine better."

"Ever hire your guns out?"

Dundee scowled. "You got somebody you want killed, you just go and shoot him yourself. I do honest work."

He thought he saw a flicker of a smile across Titus' face, and a look of satisfaction. "I'm sure you do, Dundee. What I had in mind would be honest. I wouldn't lie to you, though. It's so damned honest it just *could* get you killed."

"How's that?"

"Where I want you to go, honest men are as rare as fresh peaches in January. They're in open season the year around."

"If somebody was to shoot me, I don't see where that money of yours would do me any good."

"I got a notion you can take care of yourself. Anyway, man, think of the challenge."

"I'm not a schoolboy. A challenge don't stir me anymore."

"But I'll bet money does."

Dundee took the bottle and poured himself a fresh drink. "You got the money; I got the time. Long as your whisky holds out, I'll at least listen. What's your problem?"

"Cowthieves. Hideburners. They're after me like heelflies after an old bull. I need them stopped."

"Why don't you just call in the Texas Rangers? That's their line of work."

"It's *my* cattle; I'll pay for my own remedies. Man runs to the government with all his trouble, it's a sign of weakness. When I itch, I scratch for myself."

Or hire somebody to do the scratching for you, Dundee thought. "How come you think I'm the man to do it for you? You don't know me. For all you know, *I* could be a cowthief." He grunted. "For all *I* know, I *could* be one, if the profit looked big enough."

Titus shook his head. "You're not one of that kind. Some people are easy to read, minute you set eyes on them. I got a strong notion you could go down into that den of snakes and bite as hard as *they* do."

"Where is this snake den?"

"You ever been down in the Llano River country, south of here?"

Dundee said he hadn't. Titus said, "It's rough country, lots of brush and timber. A regular outlaw paradise. They even got a town of their own, if you'd *call* it a town . . . a place by the name of 'Runaway.' Ever hear of it?"

Dundee shook his head. "Never even heard of Titusville till I rode in here."

"Runaway's not on any map. It's just down there, like a boil on a man's backside. It's outside of this county. Local sheriff's got no jurisdiction down there, and what's more, he don't want any. Runaway's a far piece from its own county seat, and they don't even keep a deputy there. Bad climate, hard on your health."

"Looks like the thing to do is just to hire you a couple or three dozen gunslingers, go down there and clean house. Be done with it once and for all."

"I will. But I got to go about it right. Old days, a man could just go down and throw a nice, big hanging party and burn the damned place and be shed of it, and no questions asked. But now people have got awful righteous about things like that. They get upset and call for investigations and such . . . cause a heap of bother. Anyway, I'm not a hard man, Dundee. There's some good people down there—a few, at least—and I don't want to have to hurt them all just to get at the heelflies. Trouble is, I don't know just who-all's doing the stealing. That'd be one of the things I'd want you to find out. Once I know the guilty ones, I'll get me some men and go down there and throw one hell of a good party.''

Dundee's opinion of Titus was slowly on the rise. Some cowmen he knew would simply ride down on such a town like a cyclone, sweep it clean and tell God they'd all just died.

"Titus, you're a wealthy man. A few cowthieves won't break you."

"No?" Titus clenched a big fist on the table. Dundee could tell by the rough look of it that it had known a long lifetime of hard work. "You've heard the old saying: the bigger a man is, the harder he goes down. I got debts, Dundee, debts that would scare old Jim Fisk himself. The cattle I'm losing can be the difference between me hanging on and going under. I got to stop the leaks, and I will. I want to do it the right way: get the people who are hurting me and leave the innocent folks alone. But if I wind up with my back to the wall, I'll take desperate measures. I *will* go down there and wipe the whole slate clean. When a man comes up to the snubbing post, he's got to save himself."

"And what about the innocent ones?"

"I expect there was a few good people in Jericho, Dundee. But when Joshua blew that trumpet, they all went down."

Dundee shrugged. It wasn't any skin off of his nose, one way or the other. But he had a feeling he could get to like this Titus, if he stayed around. Dundee liked contrary men, too. "You asked me if I'd ever hired out my guns. I have, but only when I liked the deal."

"I'm not asking you to go down there and kill out all them varmints. I'm not asking you to kill *anybody*, unless there comes a need for it. I just want you to go find out who's running off my stock. I'll handle it from there. I'll pay you more than you could make in two years if you was to try to earn it cowboying.''

Dundee thought about Titus' hotel, and the beds in it, and the colored wallpaper. "How much in advance?"

"Say, two hundred dollars. The balance when you get back.''

"What if I don't *get* back?''

"Then I save the rest of the money.'' Titus let a tiny smile flicker, then go out. "I'll be square with you, Dundee. I've sent two men down there already. One of them acted like a broke cowpuncher riding the chuckline. Figured that would give him a chance to see a lot. They dumped his body in the street here one night, right in front of my *ho*tel. The other one went down there acting like a cattle buyer. I never *did* see him again.''

Dundee reached for the bottle, then changed his mind. He could already feel a glow starting. If he was going to dicker on a deal, he didn't want any cobwebs on his brain. "Saying I was to decide to go down there, I don't intend to do it acting like somebody I ain't. Been times in my life I ain't told all there was to the story, but there's never been a time I ever out-and-out lied about anything. I won't make any big point of it, but if anybody asks me, my name is Dundee and I'm working for you. No lies, no play-acting.''

Titus shrugged. "How you do it is up to you. I just want to be damn sure it gets done.''

Son Titus stepped through the door. He had washed the blood from his face and dusted his clothes a little. But around one eye a blue spot the size of a half dollar was beginning to show up. And one cheek was skinned down to the color of calf meat. Dundee nodded in satisfaction. It had always pleasured him to see a job well done.

Son Titus said suspiciously, "Pa, what you talking to this drifter about?''

Titus stirred in annoyance. "Nothing that's any concern of yours. Go find yourself something to do, and this time leave that knife in your pocket.''

"There ain't nothing to do, Pa, and you know it. You don't allow no high-stepping women in Titusville, or no high-limit poker games. Anyhow, I wouldn't ask you if I didn't want to know. What you getting mixed up with this stranger for?"

"Hiring him for a little job of work, is all. Go play marbles, or something."

Dundee judged Son Titus to be about twenty-one or two, somewhat beyond the age for marbles.

Son said, "I heard a little of it from the porch. You're sending him to Runaway, ain't you? You think maybe he's going to catch them cowthieves." The young man answered his own question with a show of contempt. "He won't. He'll take whatever you give him, then go down there and join up with them. That is, if that's not where he come from in the first place. I can tell by the look of him. I bet you a million dollars he's a cowthief himself."

Dundee slowly got to his feet. He clenched a fist, wincing as pain lanced through a battered knuckle. "Boy, if you keep working at it, you're finally going to make me take a disliking to you."

John Titus said, "Son Titus, you get along out of here. You haven't *got* a million dollars, and you never will. You haven't got much sense sometimes, either."

"I got sense enough to take care of that Runaway job for you, if you'd let me. You don't have to go hiring some drifter."

The father's voice was sharp. "Son Titus, if you don't want to spend all this summer roundup jingling horses and holding the cut, you better do what I tell you."

Son Titus turned and walked out talking to himself. He paused on the porch, looking back, his eyes hot with resentment.

John Titus said, and not without pride, "He's contrary. I reckon that's why I like him."

Only a father could, Dundee thought. *And maybe a mother.* He settled back into his chair. "If I was to take this job, you got any ideas where I ought to start at?"

"I'll give you the names of some people I think are honest. And I'll tell you about a few of the other kind. Main name to begin with, I think, is old Blue Roan."

"What kind of a name is *that*?"

"It's the name of a cowthief, the daddy of them all. Smart as a mustang, mean as a one-eyed polecat. Whatever you find down there, I expect old Roan Hardesty is at the center of it."

"Sounds like you know him."

"I do. Long time ago, down in deep South Texas, him and me used to steal cattle together." Titus paused, seeing surprise in Dundee's eyes. "Hell yes, I used to steal cattle. How else do you think I got my start? We all did, them days. But I reformed. Blue Roan never did."

Titus sat in silence, waiting. "Well, how about it, Dundee? You want to take the job?"

Dundee bit off the end of a cigar and then lighted a match. He drew, getting the tobacco worked up to a glow.

"The beds in that *ho*tel of yours . . . they good and soft?"

II

In the 1880s, much of the Texas hill country which shed its waters into the Llano River, and down into the Frio and the Nueces, was known far and wide as thieves' territory, for it was a big land of high, rough hills, of rocky ranges, of deep valleys and heavy, protective timber—liveoak, Spanish oak, cedar and mesquite—of hundreds of clear-water springs and dozens of creeks and streams—of the Llanos themselves, the North, the South and the main Llano. Here great herds of cattle could be swallowed up and lost. Bold men could make fortunes in the light of the moon by the ambitious use of long ropes and fast horses, fanning out in all directions to take other men's cattle, other men's horses, bringing them here to this favored land of strong grass and abundant water, far from law, far from the harsh hand of retribution.

Riding the bay, leading a packhorse lent him by John Titus, Dundee took his time heading south and west into the Llano River country. Carrying a generous amount of Titus grub in his pack, and *most* of two hundred dollars in his pocket—that hotel had overcharged him—he saw no reason to be in a hurry. He doubted the cowthieves would leave before he got there.

He took a long, leisurely look at the Titus cattle he came across. He decided they weren't different from most other people's. Some places, cowmen had brought in improved bulls such as the imported Shorthorn to start a gradual upgrading. Titus still held onto the pure Longhorn, the native Texas "mustang" breed. The only visible step toward improvement was that he had steered all the male produce except the ones he had selected as best—and the ones he couldn't catch. The latter bequeathed a certain hardihood to their progeny, whatever shortcomings they might have had as beef. Some of the Titus bulls showed strong Mexican blood, and even beyond that, the fighting strains that went back to ancient Spain. Most range cattle fought horsemen only when provoked. Twice Dundee found bulls coming to meet him halfway, pawing their challenge.

He guessed Titus liked his cattle contrary too.

One thing he noted was the form of the Titus T Bar brand, made with three stamps of a straight bar iron, the bar under the T. Every time Dundee sat awhile on the ground, whether to eat, rest the horses or just ease his tired rump, he would take a stick and draw the T Bar in the dirt. Then he would start improvising various ways it could be burned over with a running iron and converted into something else. He was amazed at the many variations. He could join the T to the bar and then cross a line through it and make a Double E. He could run the upright through the top of the T and make a Cross Bar. He could make a Double Cross, a TE, a TF Bar, a Big I, a Rocking R, a JE. There was little limit other than a man's ingenuity, and

Dundee had observed that when it came to thievery, many a dull man was transported into genius.

John Titus must surely know his brand was easy to alter. Its lines were too simple. If he would use something complicated, after the Mexican style, he would present the hideburners a challenge. But this was probably a measure of the man's stubbornness. The brand was *his*. He would hang onto it come hell or high losses.

As he drew the various brands that he could conceive from the T Bar, Dundee catalogued them in his mind. As far as he was concerned, any cattle he came across with such a brand belonged to Titus.

The country became rougher and brushier, the farther he went south. He never was sure when he passed beyond the boundaries of the Titus ranch. Actually, he knew Titus didn't own more than a fraction of the land he used. What he had done—what a great many early Texas cowmen had done when the land showed signs of settling up—was to buy or lease all the land he could get that had natural water on it. The man who controlled the water thus controlled all the land within a cow's practical walking distance of it, for the land was valueless without water. A dry ranch up in the hills wasn't worth the shirt on a man's back. Dundee figured that a map of Titus' deeded land would be little more than a map of springs, creeks and streams. It was legal enough, and ingeniously simple. Dundee didn't begrudge him his holdings. He only regretted that he hadn't gotten here early enough to do the same thing himself.

The breaks of the game, he reasoned. *Them as has, gits.*

He found awesomely-twisted gray-green liveoaks edging the shell-studded limestone hills, and Mexican cedars growing in dense brakes, single cedars dotting the hills all the way to the rimrocks. There was often a tangly type of underbrush in the valleys, rustling with the wind and with the unseen movement of animals and rodents and Lord knew what. Now and again he would catch a glimpse of a big rack of horns an instant before a whitetail buck deer darted off into the protection of the heavy sumac and Spanish oak. Once in a while he stirred up a few wild turkeys, which sprinted away like racehorses, or flew up explosively like the bob-white quail. Once the bay snorted and jumped and almost lost him as a long-nosed, thick-plated armadillo scurried out from underfoot.

Good country for wild animals, Dundee thought. *No wonder it appeals to wild men.*

The first scattered bunch of cattle he found in the roughs were standing around a half-dried waterhole in a rocky draw. He rode up on them quietly and with care. He managed to see the brands before the first old cow jerked her head up high, took one good look at him and went clattering off for the thickets. The rest followed close behind her, their tails up, their dignity injured.

Most of them carried what he took to be a Rocker M, or maybe it was meant for a Hat. Either way, it wasn't a conversion from the T Bar. However, Dundee saw one which looked suspicious. Best he could tell in the second or two he'd had a view, it was a box with a straight line down through it. That one could very easily have been made over from the Titus brand. He took a small tally book from his pocket and sketched the brand as he had seen it. He recorded the Rocker M, too, just for reference. As he went along, tallying every brand, he would begin to find out who claimed each one. There would come a time, someday, for a reckoning.

He spent long days quietly riding out the creeks and streams as he came across them, noting brands, jotting each new one in the book, sketching a rough map. During that time he found at least half a dozen brands which could have been—and most probably were—the illegitimate offspring of the T Bar.

Somewhere he had read about the big fish living off of the little ones. Here it looked more like the little ones living off of the big.

Dundee studiously avoided people. Now and again he would see a picket cabin or a small rock house or even a tent pitched somewhere close to water, with perhaps a few brush corrals and a rude barn or two. These he observed at length and committed to map and memory, but he didn't go down for a talk.

He found few cattle carrying the Titus brand. That, he

thought, was a little odd. Even with Titus riders patrolling the outer edges of what Titus considered to be his rightful range, it seemed probable that on an outfit so large, some cattle would naturally stray out of bounds. It was to be expected. Seemed like the bigger the ranch, the farther the cattle wandered.

Dundee figured they wandered, all right, and probably a good many were encouraged more than somewhat. Any strays which showed up this far from home likely didn't carry the T Bar very long. It would be converted into something else in no more time than it took somebody to get a fire going and an iron hot.

One morning, moving the bay and the packhorse down a ridge, he heard cattle bawling. He paused to listen. From the sound of it he knew they were being driven. A cow bawling for a strayed calf sounds one way. Bawling of a cow forcibly separated from a calf under stress sounds another. And the bawling of many cows at one time means a herd being moved. Dundee eased into the protection of a cedar motte and waited patiently, smoking himself a leisurely cigarette.

In due time the cattle came into sight. At a distance he estimated seventy or eighty head. As they gradually came nearer, he counted about fifty cows and twenty-five or thirty calves. Dundee reached into his saddlebag and brought out a small spyglass Titus had lent him. It was too far yet to read the brands and earmarks, so he studied the four riders. Best he could tell, the one in charge was a tall, heavy man in a Mexican sombrero. At least he seemed to be giving orders, what few were being given. These men knew their business without needing much instruction. It occurred to Dundee they were moving the cattle too fast, though. No bigger than this bunch was, if they would let the cows set their own pace, the calves would keep up with their mammies and there wouldn't be all this bawling. A real cowman wouldn't push his own cattle this way except for a short distance. These had been walking a long time. They had a trail-drawn look about them.

The riders were putting the cattle across a nice grassy flat, one of the best Dundee had seen this side of the T

Bar. Most of the cattle he had found in this region carried the Rocker M, or the Hat, or whatever it was. A little before sundown yesterday Dundee had scouted what appeared to be the headquarters, on up about three or four miles beside a nice spring. He had sat on the brow of a hill and looked down with the spyglass for an hour or more, studying the layout. A double cabin there, built of logs, was better constructed than most he had seen. Whoever these people were, they had built with every intention of staying. He had seen a picket saddleshed and a set of corrals, part of them built of brush and some of stone, laboriously stacked.

A couple of times he had seen a woman. At the distance he couldn't tell much about her. She was small, and by the ease of her movements he guessed she was young. He hadn't seen any children. About sundown two horsemen had come in from somewhere above, had unsaddled their horses and put the saddles in the shed. One man was a bit heavy and moved with the stiffness of age. The other had the movements of a young man, and the energy. While the older of the two limped slowly to the cabin and flopped beneath a brush arbor to rest, the younger strode to a pile of rocks beside the corral and carried several to the fence he was building, setting them in place. He didn't stop until the woman came out and waved him to supper. About that time Dundee had decided he was hungry too, so he had pulled back a safe distance and made camp.

He had thought about that stone fence some as he sat around his own campfire, chewing venison and sipping boiled coffee. Stone fences and laziness didn't go together.

He noted that none of the riders pushing these cattle sat their horses like the two he had observed yesterday. Eventually the small herd came close enough that with the spyglass he could read the brands. Most of the calves were still slick-eared, but the cows weren't. They belonged to Titus.

Sitting there, Dundee tried again to study out a way the T Bar could be altered into the Rocker M. It couldn't be done.

This don't add up, he thought. *I reckon I'll just follow along*.

As he was fixing to ride out from the motte, he hauled up short. Three riders were coming from the south. Another minute and he would have been in their view. They came upon the trail of the cattle, paused a moment and followed the tracks. Dundee scratched his head, wondering. He decided to stay on the higher ground and see without being seen. Some games, it was better to watch than to play in.

Presently the three riders overtook the cattle. They howdied and shook with the drovers and sat their horses in a circle, taking time to smoke and parley. One man rode off. Before long he came back, pointing.

Across the big flat, from the southwest, a rider pushed along in an easy trot. Dundee dismounted with the spyglass. He could recognize people sometimes by the way they sat their horses. He knew this was the man he had observed yesterday working on the corral.

Three men peeled away from the herd and rode to intercept the rider. Dundee could see angry gestures. At length the heavy man in the Mexican sombrero turned back and spoke to the two who sat a little behind him. The heavy man held a pistol. The two men dismounted slowly, deliberately, and walked to the fence-builder's horse. One reached up and grabbed. The horseman slid out of the saddle, and they sprawled together in the dust. The two set in to beat him with their fists.

The other man abandoned the cattle and spurred up to watch the fight. They formed a semi-circle around the sombreroed horseman who had done their initial arguing and had given the orders. The breeze brought Dundee their shouts of encouragement.

Though it was two against one, the lone man put up a good fight of it, for a while. Toting those rocks had put a good set of muscles on him, Dundee reasoned. One of the two who was beating him finally stretched out on the ground and didn't get up. The heavy man ordered fresh blood into the fray.

The unequal contest raised a resentful anger in Dundee, and he considered going down there. But the odds were too long. There were too many guns. He reasoned that if they had intended to kill the man, they would have done it at the start.

Anyway, it wasn't any of his put-in.

The fence-builder didn't have the chance of a one-legged pullet in a coyote den, but he resisted with all he had. Wearying, he swayed, staggered, swung without strength. Someone's fist hit him every time he opened up. He went down, pushed to his feet, went down again, came up as far as his knees, got struck in the jaw and went down to stay. The man in the sombrero dismounted and delivered him a couple of hard kicks in the ribs. Gritting his teeth, Dundee held the spyglass on that man long enough to decide he wasn't a Mexican, despite the hat.

You got something coming to you, hoss, Dundee thought. *I hope I'm there when it's delivered.*

The leader pointed back to the slowly-scattering herd. The horsemen grudgingly turned away from the downed fighter and trailed in a ragged line to the cattle. After a bit they drove the cows and calves by the beaten man, and on beyond him.

Even in the shade, the close heat was oppressive here in the cedars, where the thin breeze could not move through the dense foliage. Dundee wondered about that man down yonder, sprawled on the ground in the open sun. *Least they could do was drag him to the shade.* His impulse was to go on down and help, but he made himself wait until the cattle passed over a rise and out of view.

The lone man heard him coming. He raised up onto hands and knees, defiance in his eyes. He reached back to his hip, but they had thrown his pistol away into the grass.

Dundee raised his hand in the peace sign. "I don't mean you no harm." The young man tried to push to his feet. Dundee said: "Wait and I'll help you. Go slow. If they've busted anything, you don't want to lose the pieces."

The man swayed. His face was bloody and torn, his beribboned shirt crusted with dust and sweat. His hands were laced and bleeding.

Dundee said, "They done a right smart of a job on you."

The man licked his bleeding lip. "Where'd my horse go?"

"He run off. That's the way with horses." Dundee hunted around till he found the pistol and returned it.

"You gave them a good fight."

A suspicious gaze bore into Dundee. "Who are you?"

"You wouldn't know me. Name's Dundee."

"You saw the fight?"

"Had me a spyglass."

"And you didn't do a thing to help me?"

Dundee shrugged. "I spent a lot of money across a poker table before I learned there's no use going against a stacked deck. Figured your health was lost anyway and I'd keep mine so I could come down here and put the pieces back together." He jerked his thumb toward the bay. "Think you can get on my horse? I'll take you to the creek. You'll feel better once you wash the dirt and blood off."

Dundee had to help him into the saddle, then swung up behind the cantle and sat on the bay's hips. "I'd as soon not have to keep calling you '*You*.' You got a name?"

"McCown. Warren McCown."

McCown. That would fit with the Rocker M brand.

Dundee squatted patiently on his heels and flipped rocks into the creek while McCown stripped off his clothes and waded into the water. He noted that McCown's face, neck and hands were brown, but the rest of his body was white. Most early cowboys buttoned their collars and their sleeves. They believed it was cooler if you kept the sun out, the skin covered.

McCown soaked till the dirt and blood were washed away.

Lord help the fish, Dundee thought.

Now that he could see the cowboy's face plainer, he judged him to be in his late twenties. Presently McCown came out and sat on the gravelly bank to let the wind dry him. "Feel better?" Dundee asked.

McCown only nodded.

"Some of them marks didn't wash off. You'll carry them a spell." McCown still only nodded. Dundee said, "You sore about me not coming down and throwing in with you?"

McCown shrugged. "You didn't know me."

"I still don't."

McCown glanced at him sharply. "And *I* don't know *you*. I do know that packhorse is carrying a T Bar brand on him. You steal him?"

Dundee's eyes narrowed. "Make any difference to you if I did?"

"I got worries enough of my own. Old Titus can watch out for himself."

Dundee reflected a moment. "Who *were* them jolly lads you was entertaining back there?"

McCown stared him straight in the eye. "While ago you didn't want to get involved. You'd better just stay clear of it all around. What you don't know won't cause you no trouble."

McCown put on his hat first, then his long underwear, then his boots, his remnant of a shirt, and his trousers. "Mind letting me ride double with you to my cabin? Ain't far."

"I know where it is."

When McCown showed surprise, Dundee said: "I know more than you think I do. I know you got a log cabin and brush pens and you're building yourself a set of rock corrals. I know you got an old man living with you, and a wife."

McCown's eyes narrowed, but he held his tongue.

Dundee said: "What's more, I know you brand a Rocker M, and that there ain't no way to make a Rocker M out of a T Bar. I already tried."

"Who the hell *are* you?"

"Told you, my name's Dundee."

"A man can change names like he changes shirts. A name don't mean nothing."

"I'm working for John Titus. I come to see what's been doing with his cattle."

"And you been watching me, figuring me for a thief."

"Not necessarily. I thought you *might* be."

"Now you figure I'm not?"

"Not necessarily. Mount up. I'll ride behind again."

"I think I'd as soon walk as ride with a man who thinks I'm a thief."

"I ain't said you are, and I ain't said you're not. I got a wide open mind. Now, if you want to ride home, you better get up on that horse."

They moved up the creek in an easy trot, McCown silently nursing his resentment, Dundee making no apology and, indeed, not even considering the possibility that he should. To him, apology was a sign either of weakness or of being wrong, and he seldom conceded either.

A mile or so from headquarters, he saw a rider approaching, leading a horse. "Hope this is a friend of yours, McCown."

McCown squinted. "It's Uncle Ollie. He's bringing my horse."

An elderly man slouched gracelessly in the saddle, taking his time. His face furrowed in concern, though worry didn't seem to enhance his speed. "Horse come in without you, Warren. Millie like to've had a fit." He cocked his head over. "Look at you! I been telling you this horse'd throw you off."

"It wasn't the horse, Uncle Ollie. It was. . . ." He turned half around to look at Dundee. "I run into some boys back yonder."

"Was old Blue Roan with them?"

Dundee listened intently, remembering what Titus had said about Roan. McCown frowned. "I didn't say it was Roan's bunch."

"They marked you, boy, they surely did. They'll kill you, you don't watch out." The old man turned his squinting attention to Dundee, his eyes light gray, set against a sun-darkened skin wrinkled and dried like neglected leather. "And who might you be?"

McCown answered for Dundee. "You can call him the silent observer."

Dundee said, "The name's Dundee."

The old man reached out, his grip casual. "Mine's Ollie McCown."

To dismount without Dundee's having to get down first, McCown threw his right leg over the bay's neck and jumped to the ground. Weaker than he thought, he went to his hands and knees. He straightened. "I do thank you, Dundee, for what help you *have* been. Maybe I'll get to do the same for you sometime . . . if I'm real lucky." There was a touch of malice in it. McCown took the reins from his uncle's hands and swung onto his own horse. Then a thought struck him. "How come you home when my horse came in, Uncle Ollie? You were supposed to be out rocking up that spring on the south branch."

The old man shrugged like a kid caught at mischief. "I got tired. Anyway, I thought it'd be nice to go down to the creek and catch a nice mess of fish for Millie to fix for supper."

McCown grumbled: "You and that fishing pole! I'd burn it, but you'd just fix another."

Glad I don't work for him, Dundee thought. *All he lacks is a whip.*

Dundee noticed Uncle Ollie looking with concern at the brand on the packhorse. Warren McCown saw, too. "Dundee works for John Titus. He's down here to find out where the Titus cattle are going."

The old man said, "Reckon people might think we're taking sides with him, Warren?"

"Let them."

"They done beat you up. Next time they might kill you!"

"This is my place, and I'll do as I please on it." McCown turned to Dundee. "Since you're this close, you might as well come and have supper. I owe you that much for the ride."

"Much obliged." Dundee decided if he kept his mouth shut and his ears open, he might learn something. And even if he didn't learn anything, he'd get something in his belly besides old bacon and gamy venison and poor coffee and promises. If a man couldn't get rich—and Dundee doubted he ever would—the next best thing was to get fat.

There was nothing elaborate about the McCown place, for this was not a country given to fancy things. Poor for pretty but hell for stout. They passed the incomplete stone corrals, and the piles of wagon-hauled rocks which one day would find their place in the fences. The stones had been selected for size and shape up in the hills, more than likely, through long, hot days of back-breaking toil.

McCown pointed to a finished rock corral in which stood the saddlesheds. "You can put your horses in there and feed them. You'll likely want to be a-riding again come morning."

Dundee carried his saddle into the shed and set it across a rack that was simply a smoothed-off log placed atop a pair of posts. He noted that the shed's walls were upright cedar pickets, axe-hewn for a close fit and set well into the ground to hold them solid. The roof was tightly built of liveoak timbers, cedar and sod.

Another contrary man, Dundee thought. He'd have to be to drive himself to this kind of work.

Somehow Dundee thought McCown might have oats for his horses, but instead the rancher dug into a barrel and came up with dried mesquite beans. Well, what they lacked in feed value, they made up in convenience. And they didn't cost anything.

McCown paused at the gate and looked toward the unfinished rock fence. "I reckon I'll come back out here after supper and work till dark. Don't lack too much finishing me another pen."

Uncle Ollie said: "After that beating you got? You better go to bed, Warren McCown."

A woman stood in the open dog-run that separated the two sections of the cabin. Moving in that direction, walking to the right of the hobbling Uncle Ollie, Dundee found himself studying her. She was slender; he could tell that at a distance. Nearer, he could see she was younger than he had thought, watching at a distance through the spyglass. Now he could see her long brown hair, strands of it lifting in the wind, strands that when down to full length must reach nearly to her waist. She had a thinnish oval face, not yet sun-hardened but still clean and soft. It was a natural face, one that probably had never known powder or rouge or any form of lip-reddening like the town women sometimes used.

The young woman—she might have been twenty or so—gasped at sight of McCown's face. "Warren. . ."

McCown gestured that it didn't amount to anything. "You about got supper ready? I want to do a little more work before it gets too late."

Uncle Ollie shrugged in futility.

The woman turned to stare at Dundee in curiosity and, perhaps, a touch of fear. Dundee ran his hand over his face and realized his whiskers hadn't felt a razor since he had left Titusville. Moreover, he was dusty and streaked with grime and woodsmoke. To her, he must look like some robber chieftain, some brigand out of employ.

Dundee ventured, "I know I appear fearsome, ma'am, but I got a good heart."

Warren McCown added drily: "And a good appetite too, I expect. We may just as well feed him some of Uncle Ollie's fish."

The woman glanced at Uncle Ollie and began to smile. The old man said to Dundee, "We had it made up that if Warren raised cain about me fishing instead of working on that spring, we'd say it was Millie caught them."

Looked like nobody was going to introduce him, so he would have to do it for himself. "Mrs. McCown, my name is Dundee."

She smiled shyly. Dundee suspected the beard still worried her. "I'm Millie McCown. And it's not Mrs.; it's *Miss*."

Warren McCown said in a small triumph: "You see, you didn't know everything after all, Dundee. She's my sister, not my wife."

Dundee let it pass. A man was entitled to a small mistake now and again. For no reason he would have admitted to himself, he was somehow pleased to find she was unmarried.

The kitchen was the biggest room in the double cabin. On one wall stood a black Charter Oak stove. At a time when most people in Western Texas still cooked in an open fireplace, this was an uncommon luxury worth a dozen head of cattle or several fair-to-middling horses. A wood-box beside it was heaped full with mesquite and oak wood, chopped to length. The fish was sizzling in a deep iron skillet. Millie McCown had set three chipped plates on a plain wooden table. Now, allowing for Dundee, she set a fourth. Waiting, Dundee looked around at the plain lumber shelves, the homemade rawhide-and-cedar chairs, the two cots that would be Warren's and Uncle Ollie's. The place was built for utility. The stove was the only thing in it that would sell for three pieces of Mexican silver.

On a shelf Dundee saw an old tintype propped against a big family Bible. It pictured two soldiers in what appeared to be Confederate uniforms. One, he realized, was Uncle Ollie. This had been a good many years ago.

Ollie McCown said: "That's me on the left. I was still full of vinegar, them days. I ain't changed much in looks, just the vinegar has about run out." Dundee glanced at the old man. If Ollie didn't think he'd changed, he hadn't stood close to a mirror lately. The old man said: "That other feller, that's my brother George, the daddy of Millie and Warren. He's gone now. We buried him a long ways back."

"I'm sorry," Dundee said, and he meant it.

Dundee approached the fish with some uncertainty. He'd been seeing them in the clear-water streams and wished he could catch some, but he'd never lived in a part of the country where there were creeks to fish in. He didn't know how to start. Even if he had caught any, he wouldn't have known whether to skin them like a beef or eat them with the hide on.

Dundee found himself looking at the girl through supper, cutting his eyes away when she glanced in his direction. He knew she was aware of his staring, for once her face reddened a little. She'd been sheltered, this girl.

After supper, Warren McCown did just what he said he would do; he went out and stacked rock for the fence, despite the soreness, despite his bruises. Dundee thought he owed it to him to help, but McCown shook his head when Dundee picked up the first stone. "Wrong shape, wrong size for the tie I'm making here. I can do it better by myself.''

Dundee dropped the rock and left McCown to handle the job all by his lonesome. He walked down to the saddleshed, rubbing his beard and looking back at the cabin. He fished around in the pack for his razor and soap. He shaved in the cold water of the creek, wincing as the razor scraped. Done with it, he asked himself why he had gone to the trouble. He had no intentions to justify it. When a man courted a country girl like this Millie McCown, he had to have one thing in mind: marriage. Anything less would draw immediate rebuff from the girl and very possibly a bellyful of buckshot from an outraged father or brother.

Dundee knew marriage was not for him. His itchy feet hadn't been to the far side of all the hills yet. Temporary female companionship could be had in most any town, if the urge got so strong a man had to give in to it. It could be bought and paid for, then he could turn his back and ride away from her with no regrets, no sense of shirked responsibilities.

He had no thought of despoiling this country girl, even if there were no penalty for it. This was a man's country, good women as scarce as gold and as highly valued, to be treasured and protected from all that was thought dirty and raw and unpleasant. He subscribed to an old cowboy code that put a woman on a pedestal. She didn't leave it unless she deliberately stepped down. Unless a man had marriage in mind, he tipped his hat, as the knights of old tipped their visors, and held himself afar.

Uncle Ollie had stayed long at the table. Now he was stretched on the ground beneath the arbor, belching. The sun had gone down, and there was no longer any need for shade, but habit is a slavemaster. Dundee joined him, sitting on the ground, crossing his legs. Ollie's eyes narrowed as he studied Dundee's shaven face. ''Don't expect you'd win no prize, but you look a *little* better. You still got a dab of soap under your left ear.''

Dundee wiped it off onto his sleeve. He pointed his chin

toward the distant figure of Warren McCown, working in the dusk. "Is he thataway all the time?"

Ollie nodded. "He expects a lot out of a man, but he drives hisself the most of all."

"What's his hurry? Nobody gets out of this world alive."

"Maybe it was seeing his old daddy die without a dollar in his pocket, hardly. This here place is Warren's . . . his and Millie's, anyway. He's worked for it and fought for it. It's like a fever in him. I ain't sure sometimes whether Warren owns the land or the land owns him."

Millie McCown walked out into the dog-run, drying her hands on a cloth. Dundee pushed to his feet and took off his hat, bowing slightly, awkwardly. She smiled, and he sensed she was pleased he had taken time to shave. He noticed she had brushed her long hair. He wanted to pay her a compliment, but he didn't know what to say.

She said: "You don't have to get up for me. Please, be comfortable."

Dundee fetched her a rawhide chair from against the house. Then he stepped back beside Uncle Ollie and once more seated himself upon the ground. Dundee watched the girl until he knew she was nervously aware of his eyes. He looked away.

She said, "It's a nice, cool evening after such a warm day."

Dundee thought a man could hardly argue with a statement like that. "Yes, ma'am."

"Maybe it'll be the same again tomorrow."

"I expect."

"It was like this yesterday."

"Yes, ma'am."

A long silence followed. But Dundee could see Millie McCown's lips working a little. She was biting them, working up nerve to ask him: "Mister Dundee, I couldn't get Warren to tell me what happened to him, how he got so skinned up and bruised. Will *you* tell me?"

Dundee hesitated. If McCown wanted her to know, he would have told her.

"Please, Mister Dundee?"

The pleading tone of her voice melted him like butter. McCown *ought* to have told her. "I don't know who the men was, ma'am. They was driving a herd of cattle that sure as he . . . heck didn't belong to them. Your brother rode up, and a fight started."

"Maybe they were our cattle."

"No, ma'am, they was carrying the T Bar, old John Titus' brand." Maybe no one had told her. "I work for John Titus."

She nodded. "Oh. And you were trailing the cattle to see where they were being taken."

"That's about it, ma'am."

"And you helped my brother."

He squirmed. "I ain't fixing to lie to you; I didn't get in the fight. But later I went down and done what I could."

"If I know Warren, he didn't even think to thank you. So *I* thank you, Mister Dundee."

"No trouble, ma'am. I'd of done as much for a broken-legged dog." He rubbed his neck. *That* hadn't come out the way he meant it.

She seemed not to notice. "It was old Blue Roan, or some of his men; I'd bet on that. Warren's had trouble with them. They keep bringing cattle across our land, cattle that don't belong to them."

Uncle Ollie stirred nervously. "Millie. . . ."

She went on: "We're minding our own business, or trying to. If Roan Hardesty steals cattle, that's between him and the law, or between him and the people he takes the cattle away from. But he's got no right to drive them across our land and draw us into it. One of these days there'll come a reckoning. We don't want to be caught up in it."

Uncle Ollie's eyes were narrowed. "Millie, you better hush up and not be making loose talk. That'll get us in trouble too."

"I'm just saying what's true."

"You're saying it to a man who represents John Titus. Ain't no use having Roan and his crowd come over here some fine day and shut all of us up for good. They could do it, you know."

She said with confidence, "Warren can take care of us."

The old man grunted. "He ain't but one man. I'm only half a man, and you're no man atall. If it comes a showdown, we won't last long."

Guardedly Dundee suggested: "You wouldn't have to be alone. I think John Titus would help anybody who helps *him*."

She asked, "What kind of help could we give him?"

Dundee brought out his tally book. "I been jotting down brands. I'd be much obliged if you'd tell me who claims them."

Uncle Ollie said tightly: "Dundee, I was in the big war. I didn't own no slaves; it wasn't none of my business. But I got in it anyway. All I got for it was a hole in my leg and some sense in my head. I learned one thing; take care of your own self and stay out of a fight any way you can. Us McCowns, we're not messing into John Titus' trouble. We don't owe John Titus nothing."

"If I tell him you helped me, he might figure he owes *you* something."

"So might Blue Roan." The old man gritted, "Dundee, you go riding down into old Roan's backyard and you may not ever *see* John Titus again."

III

Dundee had seen ranches where it didn't take long to spend the night, but this place was extreme. McCown was up and stirring two hours before good daylight. Dundee had spread his blankets outdoors, beneath the arbor. Through the open window he could hear McCown poking a fire into life in the big cookstove and fussing at Uncle Ollie to rouse his lazy bones and get his clothes on so Millie could come in from her side of the cabin and start breakfast. Dundee dressed in the dark, hiding himself beneath the blanket until he had his pants on.

McCown put in an hour of work on the fence before breakfast. Dundee felt he ought to do something to pay for the hospitality, so he jerked an axe loose from the chopping block and cut stovewood until Millie McCown called the men in.

They ate hurriedly, McCown impatient to get on with work. Nobody talked much. Dundee stole glances at the girl by lamplight.

The sun came up. McCown blew out the lamp to save coal oil. "Well, Dundee, Uncle Ollie and I have got work to do, and I expect you're anxious to be on your way."

As a matter of fact, Dundee wasn't, for he kind of liked sitting here looking at the girl. But he knew an invitation to leave when he heard one. "I reckon. I got a right smart of ground to cover."

He was behind the saddleshed, lashing down the pack when he heard horses. He glanced cautiously around the cedar-stake wall. Five riders were nearing the cabin. A heavy-set old man with a hunch to his shoulders raised a big hand, and the riders stopped. The old man rode on a couple more yards. His voice was deep and loud and carried well in the cool morning air.

"McCown, I came to parley with you."

Warren McCown stepped out onto the small porch, followed by a cringing Uncle Ollie. Both had six-shooters strapped around their waists. Millie McCown's frightened face appeared in the doorway. Seeing her, the old man took off his floppy old hat. His gray hair sparkled like frost in the early sun. His voice seemed almost pleasant for a moment. "Morning, Miss McCown. I swear, you do get prettier every time I see you."

If she made any reply, Dundee couldn't hear it. As yet unseen, he decided to stay put awhile.

The big old man said: "Little lady, what I got to say to your brother ain't of no concern to you, and if they was any cusswords to be accidentally dropped, I wouldn't want them falling on your ears. Ain't you got some chickens to feed or a cow to milk or something?"

Millie didn't move. The old man said: "I promise you, ma'am, there's not a man here would harm a hair on your head. I'd shoot ary one that tried. Now, why don't you go on off and take care of the chores or something, so me and your brother can have us a talk?"

Warren McCown said, "Go on, Millie."

Millie McCown glanced fearfully at the men, then walked briskly toward the saddleshed. Dundee stepped out of sight, knowing the men's gaze would follow her.

When she came around the shed, Dundee put his finger to his lips. He said quietly, "I reckon that's be Blue Roan?"

She grabbed Dundee's arm. "If there's trouble, will you help my brother?" Her fingers were tight. "I'll take another look at that tallybook. I'll give you the names of all the people I know."

Right then he'd have charged hell with a bucket of water if she'd asked him to. And not for any tallybook.

He stepped to his bay and gingerly slipped the carbine up out of the scabbard. He peered around the wall. The riders had their backs turned partially to him and all their attention riveted on the McCowns. He could hear Roan Hardesty's bull voice.

"McCown, I understand you and some of my boys butted heads yesterday."

McCown only stared in defiance. Hardesty said: "Now boy, I thought you and me had come to an understanding. I told you how things was going to be. Now, they're going to *be* thataway, whether it suits your pleasure or not."

McCown gritted, "This is my land."

"You got some papers that was signed in Austin, but you're a long ways from Austin now. I was here before you ever come. I expect to stay here a long time yet. Whether you stay or not depends on you." He paused. "McCown, you got guts; I'll give you credit for that.

Now, I'm not a mean sort of a man. I don't like to have to go and get hard with anybody. And killing just ain't my idea of the right way atall. But, boy, there's an end to my patience.''

''You got no right to dictate what goes on in this whole section of the country. You're just one man,'' McCown said.

''But I got a lot of men with me. *You're* just one man, McCown. Your uncle here makes two. You don't have to have no schooling to figure out that two is an awful little number.''

Dundee thought, *And two and one makes three*. He stepped out from behind the shed, the saddlegun cradled across his left arm, one finger in the trigger guard. He walked slowly toward the horsemen, until one of them heard the jinkle of his spurs and turned, stiffening. The others saw him. Big old Roan Hardesty twisted slowly in the saddle, surprised, squinting for recognition that wouldn't come.

Dundee stopped, the rifle not pointed at anybody in particular but in a position that it could, quickly.

Hardesty stared. ''Boy, I reckon you know how to shoot that thing?''

Dundee nodded.

Hardesty sighed in resignation. ''I got a feeling you do. You some kin of McCown's?''

''Never seen him till yesterday.''

''Then how come you're siding him?''

''I owe him for breakfast.''

The old man's round face softened a little, for he seemed to find some odd kind of humor here. ''It must've been a better breakfast than the one *I* got. Don't it occur to you that you may be paying too high a price? You could be making an awful big mistake.''

''I've made a few in my time. One more won't hurt me.''

''Don't bet on it.'' The old man pointed his heavy jaw toward the men who flanked him. ''You can count, can't you? And there's plenty more where these come from. There ain't but three of you.''

Dundee said evenly: "If trouble starts, I shoot you first. It wouldn't help you none if you had a *hundred* men."

The old man shrugged. "Logic like that, there ain't no use arguing with. I never did think I'd want to die in the cool of the morning; it's too pleasant a time to leave. Boys, let's be moving on. I think McCown has got a pretty good notion what I was meaning to tell him."

The men reined about, but they did it so as to keep Dundee in view. It seemed they knew Dundee was the man to contend with, rather than McCown. Roan Hardesty edged his dappled gray horse up closer to Dundee and halted. Only then did Dundee get a good look at the aging but strong face, the full power of stern gray eyes that fastened on a man like a pair of spikes. And he saw— without being told—why they called him Blue Roan. Across the side of his face, as if flung there by an angry hand, was a scattering of large blotches, like freckles almost, except that they were blue.

"Young fellow," Roan said, "nerve is a nice thing to have, long as you don't abuse it."

"I never was noted for good sense."

"You'd best cultivate it, then, or you may not be noted for long life, either." The old man turned and rode out of the McCown yard.

Warren and Ollie McCown didn't move a toe until Hardesty's men were a good two hundred yards away. The McCown stepped down from the little porch and slowly walked to Dundee. "You didn't have to come out."

"I owed you."

"They wasn't fixing to do any shooting."

"How do you know?"

"I just know. You could've stayed put, like yesterday. Then *I* wouldn't be left owing *you*."

Dundee frowned, his patience thinning. "Does it bother you, owing somebody?"

"It chews on me like a dog worrying a bone."

"Then forget it. Like I told Hardesty, I just paid for my breakfast."

Dundee turned away sharply and left him standing there. At the saddleshed, Millie McCown waited, her face a shade whiter. She watched as he slipped the saddlegun back into the scabbard.

"Thank you, Mister Dundee."

He turned slowly, facing her. "Thank *you*, ma'am, for saying 'thanks.' You must've learned it from your old daddy. It didn't come from your brother."

"You're a good man, Mister Dundee."

"Some people would argue with that," Dundee said.

"Not with *me* they wouldn't. Now where's that tally book?"

It turned out she didn't know but a couple of the brands. She didn't get away from this house much. But anything was good for a start. Dundee swung into the saddle, then took off his hat. "Thanks for the good meals, ma'am. They'll be long remembered."

"So will you. Come back again, when you get hungry. I'd be glad to cook some more."

"You can expect me, ma'am." He gave the lead rope a tug to bring along the packhorse. He didn't put his hat back on until he was out of the gate.

He cut across country and found the trail of the T Bar cattle still almost as plain as yesterday. Wind had begun to smooth the tracks, but he figured a blind man could still follow them, riding backwards. He moved along at a steady trot, his gaze sweeping the cedars and the liveoaks, up the valley ahead of him and back down the valley behind him. It wasn't hard to figure why the rustlers chose this route to move cattle. The grass was good and water was plentiful. They didn't have to climb up and down a lot of rocky hills. That would appeal to a lazy man. In Dundee's reckoning, the average rustler was inclined to be basically a lazy man, shunning honest work. He had little sympathy for the breed.

Hard work, he had always figured, was not something to be feared. *Avoided*, if possible, but not feared. And not avoided at the cost of making oneself an outlaw. He had seen some of the running kind through the years, always looking back over their shoulders, always wearing guns loose in their holsters, checking the back door before they trusted the front. That, he had decided long ago, was too high a price to avoid honest work. Most of the long-riders he had ever known had lived in fear, then died broke and hungry and in mortal pain. It was a coyote life . . . and death. Badly as he disliked sweat, sometimes, it was better than blood.

He came to a grassy pecan bottom where the herd evidently had been held a while to settle down and allow the cows and calves to pair. Then the cattle had been split into two bunches. One set had been pushed westward, the other south. Dundee arbitrarily chose the south.

He had to devote closer attention to the trail now, for the ground was rockier. The cattle had been moved into rougher country where limestone hills were more rugged, the postoak and cedar thicker, the grass thinner. Times he could not be sure where the driven cattle's prints stopped and loose range cattle began. He would circle and hunt till he found a horsetrack, and then he knew he was still right.

He was about to concede defeat when he heard the bawling of a calf in pain and fear. He knew the sound. He would bet the calf had been roped, or perhaps it was being branded. Drawing the saddlegun, he walked the horse slowly, watching the ground to avoid loose rocks or fallen timber. He paused every so often to listen. Now and again he heard the bawling of another calf. Each time he could tell he was closer. Afraid to crowd his luck, he finally tied the two horses and moved on afoot, cradling the carbine. He crouched to see under the low timber, and to be able to drop instantly into cover. He picked his footing carefully amid treacherous loose stones and rotted scrub brush. He climbed a hill and tried vainly to see a way down the other side that would keep him under cover. He had to backtrack partway and circle the long way around, staying well below the hill's crest to remain in the brush.

Lying on his belly, he looked down the small valley below him to cattle bunched in one end of a crude brush corral, two men and a horse with them. Every so often one of the men would climb onto the horse, swing a loop and drag a big calf by its heels. The other man would grab the calf's tail and jerk the bawling critter down on its side, then kneel on the neck and hold a foreleg. The horse would hold the rope taut and keep the animal helpless. The rider would step down, walk to a small fire and pick out a long iron. Dundee couldn't tell at the distance, but he would bet a keg of snakehead whisky that this was a running iron, designed to change brands.

He wished for the spyglass he had left in the saddlebag. He wanted to be sure about those brands. Now the only way was to move in closer. Keeping to the brush, he crept downhill toward the corral.

He stopped again, for now he saw a rude log cabin he had overlooked from up on the hill. He studied it a long time, wondering if somebody was in it. He saw no smoke curling out of the chimney. He waited, warily watching for movement. None came.

The man throwing the calves was the big rider who had been in charge of the stolen herd, the one who had seen to it that Warren McCown was beaten to the ground. He still wore that Mexican sombrero.

Dundee didn't intend to show himself. All he wanted was to get close enough to see the brands, and to get a good look at these men's faces. Intent on watching the men, he missed seeing a downed cedar. He went down sliding, sending rocks clattering, the dead cedar limb cracking like the angry strike of buckhorns.

Damn a country where a man busts his ribs on a rock!

The men ran for cover of the heavy brush fence. Almost before Dundee quit sliding, flame lanced from between logs. A bullet ricocheted off of rocks near his face.

Dundee, you've went and spilled the buttermilk again!

He was exposed, and he knew it. What he didn't know was how good a pistol shot old Mexican Hat might be. Dundee swung the saddlegun up, took reckless aim and dropped a bullet at the place he had seen the flash. The moment the woodchips flew, he sprinted for a rock the size of a washtub. A bullet whined by him, striking sparks and scattering small rocks like buckshot. Dundee fired again, taking more time to aim. He heard a howl of pain. From behind the fence he caught a frenzy of movement. At first he thought it was the cattle, stirred into panic by the firing.

Then he saw the smaller of the men jump upon the horse and spur hard, shouting. The horse went up over the low brush fence in a long leap, caught his hind feet and almost fell, straightened and went on, the rider spurring him all the way.

Dundee aimed, reconsidered and lowered the muzzle. He had never shot a man in the back, and he didn't want to cultivate any bad habits at this date. He turned his attention back to the fence.

Well, Mexican Hat, it's your move now. Do something.

He waited, but nothing happened. Impatient, Dundee aimed at the same spot where he had fired before. Once more the chips flew.

He heard a man cry weakly: "Quit your shooting. I already been hit."

"Raise up and drop your arms over this side of the fence where I can see them."

"I'm hit in the leg. I can't get up."

"You can if you want to bad enough. I want to see you before I move."

A hand showed at the top of the fence, then another, then the mashed-in, greasy sombrero, and finally a grimy, stubbled face. The big man painfully dragged himself up onto his legs—or leg, Dundee judged—and hung his arms over the fence where Dundee could see them.

Dundee pushed to his feet, the saddlegun pointed at the man. "Now, you just stand there thataway. Make one move and I'll put a bullet through the third button on that dirty shirt."

"I'm bleeding, I tell you."

"You *could* bleed a lot worse."

Dundee had forgotten the cabin in the excitement. He glanced that way again but saw no one. He cautiously approached the wounded cowthief. The man's face was rapidly draining of color. Just as Dundee reached him, the rustler's good leg gave way, and he slid slowly down on the inside of the fence.

Fearing a trick, Dundee sprinted the last three strides to the fence and shoved the carbine across. The rustler's six-shooter lay on the ground. The man wasn't going to reach for it anyway; he was all but unconscious. Dundee climbed over the fence and set the carbine against a post, where he could reach it in a hurry. He dropped to one knee. He saw a small pool of blood beneath the leg, and a spreading stain on the trousers.

"Looks like I can still shoot a little."

"Damn you," the man muttered, eyes glazing.

"You shot at me first," Dundee pointed out. "Or else your partner did. Great partner he was. Took to the tulies like a boogered rabbit."

"Damn him, too."

Dundee slit the pants leg open. The bottom of it had sealed and was holding blood like a sagging canvas holds rain. Best he could tell, the bullet had gone clean through.

"First thing we got to do is stop this bleeding, or you'll just lie here and drain your life away." He wrapped his neckerchief around the leg, above the wound. He stuck the closed pocketknife inside and used it to twist with. The flow of blood eased to a tiny trickle. "I expect you need a good shot of whisky. You got any in the cabin?" The rustler shook his head. Dundee said: "I got some on my packhorse. I'll go fetch it. Don't you run off noplace."

He saw no guns, other than the rustler's six-shooter. Examining it, he was tempted to keep it. But on reflection he decided some town-raised judge might find him guilty of theft, even though he had taken it off of a cowthief. Courts had a way of doing off-center things like that. He hurled the pistol as far as he could throw it out into the tall grass.

The cattle moved out of a corner as he crowded them a little. He saw one cow lying dead. She had caught a bullet.

It'd be like old John Titus to dock my pay by the price of that cow. What he don't know won't never hurt him.

A horse tied to a tree back of the corral had broken one leather rein in the excitement, but the other rein had held him. Dundee opened the corral gate so the cattle could wander out, then strode to the horse. It rolled its eyes at him, hinting trouble. Warily Dundee swung up and took a tight grip with his knees, expecting the horse to pitch. It humped a little, but that was all. Dundee rode him over the rocky hill, got his own two horses and came back. The rustler still lay in the same spot.

"Nice of you to stay around," Dundee said. He tilted a bottle of Titusville whisky to take a drink himself first, then handed it to the outlaw. "Here, you better have yourself a strong snort. It won't cure anything, but it'll fuzz the edges a little." He loosened the neckerchief and found the blood had almost stopped. "We better clean this wound out or you'll get an infection in it, and somebody'll have a job of digging to do, in these rocks."

He poured whisky into the bullethole.

Dundee had thought the rustler was only half conscious, but the searing of the raw whisky brought him up cursing and fighting. Dundee poured until the bottle was almost empty. Then he held it up and stared ruefully. "See there what you went and made me do? I brought this whisky along to drink, not to pour it down some cowthief. Here, you'd just as well finish what little is left."

Done with the bandage, he leaned on the fence and studied the wounded outlaw. "Your partner may not come back. He left here in an awful hurry."

"Damn him."

"If you just lay here and nobody comes, you'll likely fade away to the Unhappy Hunting Grounds. That leg'll go to gangrene."

"Damn the leg."

"I ought to just leave you, you having a penful of burnt cattle that rightfully belong to another man." Dundee frowned thoughtfully. He had never left a man alone in this kind of shape, not even a cowthief. He knew what he had to do and he regretted it, for he hadn't intended to show himself until he had finished scouting this whole Llano River country. "Seeing as I'm the one that shot you, looks like I'm duty-bound to haul you in to Runaway."

"Damn Runaway!"

In the cabin, Dundee found a lantern and a can of coal oil. He poured the oil on the floor and walls, stepped to the door and flipped a match inside.

The whole shack wasn't worth three dollars Confederate. Burning it was a gesture rather than any real damage to the cowthieves. But a man had to start someplace.

That done, he managed to get the wounded man onto his horse and head in the direction where town ought to be.

IV

The pleasant smell of woodsmoke reached him before he came over the hill, and he knew he was nearing Runaway. Dundee stopped the bay horse at the crest and looked down on the rock and log and picket houses clustered west from the sun-bright limestone face of a bluff, just back from the riverbank. He recalled John Titus' words about Runaway being not so much a town as simply a boil on a man's backside. The description was apt.

Down the valley perhaps three quarters of a mile he saw men lined up a-horseback, waving their hats and cheering. In front of them, two riders spurred and whipped their horses in a tight race, coming to the turn-around point, sliding and then spurring back to the finish line. Dundee had lost track of days, but he figured this was Sunday. Horseracing wasn't decent, except on a Sunday. Other days, a man was supposed to work.

The wounded rustler was slumped in the saddle, tied on so he couldn't slide off if he lapsed into unconsciousness. Dundee considered turning the man's horse loose here and letting it carry him on down into town where somebody would find him. But that was chancy. It would be like a fool horse to stop and graze, or even head home again, so long as the man in the saddle was unable to rein him or spur him any.

If I got it to do, I'd just as well get on with it. He led the horses down off of the hill.

Dundee had seen a few army-camp "Chihuahuas" and "scabtowns" in his time, the sort of makeshift cutthroat communities that followed in the wake of the military like scavenging dogs. This looked like one of those, except there weren't any soldiers. Studying an aimless scatter of ugly buildings—most of them saloons plain and simple—he remembered what Titus had said about there possibly being a few good people here.

Damn few, if any, Dundee judged.

The first place he came to was a wagonyard, its fence built of cedar pickets sunk into the ground and tied together at the top by strips of green rawhide. Most wagonyards had a good-sized livery barn, but not this one. Where men slept beneath the stars much of the time themselves, nobody thought of putting *horses* under a roof. The barn was nothing more than a big shed. A bewhiskered man slouched out front of an upended barrel. A considerable pile of wood shavings lay in front of him, and he was adding to it right along. He squinted at the horses and said: "It'll be two bits a head. They'll run loose in the corral. You can sleep under the shed for nothing, provided you don't get careless and set fire to the hay. That comes extra."

"I ain't trying to put the horses up. I got a man here with a bad wound in his leg. Is there a doctor in this town?"

The man got up and lazily walked around to Mexican Hat's horse. "Who is he?"

"Can't rightly say. Maybe his name is Damn. That's about the only word I been able to get out of him."

"Who shot him?"

"I did."

The stableman frowned. "Your aim ain't much good, is it?"

"I asked you if there's a doctor here."

"No doctor. Far as I know, there never was. I reckon most people here are straight-enough shots that when a man gets hit he don't need no doctor; he needs a preacher. But there ain't no preacher, neither."

"There ought to be somebody to look after a wounded man."

"You might carry him down to the Llano River Saloon. There's a woman down there pretty good at patching up after other people's sloppy shooting. Ask for Katy Long." The stableman's eyes narrowed. "Stranger here, ain't you?"

Dundee nodded.

"Well, that feller you got there, I recognize him now. He belongs to old Blue Roan. You won't be a stranger here very long." His gaze drifted to the T Bar brand on the packhorse. "I expect you got that one awful cheap."

Dundee shrugged. They'd know soon enough. "I came by him legal. I work for John Titus."

The stableman said quietly, "May you rest in peace."

Dundee took his time, studying the town as he moved along. Most of the buildings, he noted, were devoted to the sale of strong spirits and sundry types of entertainment. They ranged from little picket shacks that reminded him of a chicken crate up to one big, long structure built of stone. That one bore a small painted sign saying "Llano River Salon." They'd left an O out of the last word, but he doubted that many people noticed.

He tied the horses and said to Mexican Hat, "Don't you run off."

"Go to hell," the man mumbled.

Gratitude, Dundee reflected, had gone the way of the buffalo.

A skinny little bartender scowled. From his looks, Dundee judged that he drank vinegar instead of whisky. "What's your pleasure, friend?"

"I don't know as it *is* a pleasure. I'm looking for a woman by the name of Katy Long."

The frown didn't change. "I expect Katy is taking her siesta."

"Wake her up. I can't wait."

The frown deepened. "You been steered wrong about Katy, friend. Anyhow, there's a couple of places down the street where the girls don't ever sleep. Go try one of them."

"I got a man outside bleeding to death. I'm told she's pretty good at patching up things like that."

The bartender sighed. "She won't like it, but she'll come." He walked through a double door and down a hall. Dundee could hear him knock and call for Katy. In a moment he was back. "She'll be here directly. Let's me and you see if we can get your friend in."

A rider came jogging down the street, half asleep from some long celebration, almost bumping into the tied horses. He came awake at sight of the slumped-over man in the sombrero. "Jayce! Jason Karnes! What in hell happened to you?"

Karnes just mumbled. The rider glanced at Dundee and the bartender. "I better go tell Bunch. And Roan." He jerked the horse around and spurred into a lope toward the races.

Dundee said to the bartender: "Well, I've found out who this is. Now, who is Bunch?"

"Bunch Karnes. He's a brother to Jayce."

"Tough?"

"Mixes rattlesnake juice with his whisky."

Physically, there wasn't much strength in the little bartender. He lent moral support but not much else. Dundee supported most of the weight as they carried Karnes, dropping his sombrero in the dust. A young woman came through the double doors at the back of the room, still buttoning a high-necked dress. "Bring him on back. We'll put him on a cot and see what we can do."

She was a good-looking woman, and Dundee figured she ought to be successful in her trade. She held a door open. He brushed against her, not altogether by accident.

The woman said to the bartender: "Cricket, we'll need hot water. You better go start a fire in my cookstove."

Dundee pulled the wounded man's boots off and pitched them under the cot. "I reckon he's yours now, Katy."

She showed resentment at the familiar use of her name. "You can call me Miss Long. You don't know me, and I don't know you."

He started to say, *I know you, even if I never saw you before*. She must have seen it in his eyes. Her dislike of him was instantaneous. "You've got the wrong idea, cowboy. I make enough money selling whisky. I don't have to sell anything else." Curtly she said, "Let's see what we can do for your friend Jayce."

"He's not my friend."

"You brought him in."

"Figured I ought to. I shot him."

"Accident?"

"Not especially."

She carefully unwrapped the cloth Dundee had bound around the leg. Karnes moaned and cursed. The woman said contemptuously: "Why didn't you just go ahead and kill him? Don't you know a dirty bandage can kill a man just as dead as a bullet can?"

"I had to make do with what was there."

"Lucky thing the wound bled some and washed itself clean."

The bartender brought hot water in a pan. Katy Long cleansed the area around the wound with the skill of a trained nurse. Karnes sucked air between his teeth, but she was careful not to hurt him more than she had to.

Dundee decided to give credit where it was due. "You know your business."

"My business is whisky, and nothing else. There's no profit in this." To Karnes she said, "Grit your teeth and hang on." Karnes gripped the cotframe, his knuckles going white. He cursed and raved.

The woman glanced accusingly at Dundee. "I'm glad you had to watch."

Dundee wanted to defend himself, but pride stopped him. He didn't owe any explanation to a saloon woman. Let her think what she damn pleased.

He heard the strike of heavy boots in the hall. A gruff voice shouted: "Jayce! Where you at, Jayce?"

The woman called impatiently: "You don't have to holler. He's here."

A tall figure filled the narrow doorway. Dundee's gaze lifted to a dirty, tobacco-stained beard, to a pair of angry, blood-tinged eyes. The tall man demanded, "Who was it done this to you Jayce?"

Katy Long tried to head him off. "He'll be all right."

Dundee tensed. He knew this would be Bunch Karnes, the brother.

Karnes seemed not to hear the woman. "Jayce!" His voice was more demanding. "I said, who done this to you? I want to know."

Dundee was glad he had strapped on his pistol. He let his hands rest at his hips, handy. He suggested: "Maybe you ought to leave him be."

Hard eyes cut to Dundee's face. "What business is it of yours?"

The wounded man rasped: "He's the one done it, Bunch. He's the one shot me."

Karnes' hand dropped. Dundee brought his pistol up so fast that Karnes froze, blinking. At this range Dundee couldn't miss. Karnes swallowed.

Katy Long watched open-mouthed. For long seconds she held her breath until Karnes slowly raised his hand. Then, the moment of crisis past, she pointed to the door. "Bunch Karnes, this is *my* place, and I'm telling you to clear out. If you two have got to kill each other, do it someplace else. I don't want to clean up the mess."

The gunman's fingers flexed, his flashing eyes watching Dundee's pistol. Dundee didn't let the pistol waver from Karnes' belly. He didn't speak, for at times like this he'd never seen much gain in conversation.

Anger high in her face, the woman said sternly: "Karnes, I told you to *git!* You-all do any shooting in here, one of you is liable to hit your brother. Damn if I want to see all my work wasted."

Karnes sullenly backed toward the door. "When you come out, cowboy, I'll be waiting in the saloon."

His eyes didn't leave Dundee until he was in the hall and out of the line of vision. Dundee listened to the heavy footsteps tromping across the floor. His lungs cried out for air, and only then did he realize he had held his breath the whole time.

Katy stood in silence, her face paled.

Dundee told her, "It's all right now."

Her voice was sharp. "I don't know how you figure

that, with him waiting out yonder in the saloon. You don't know this town. You don't know people like Bunch and Jason Karnes.''

''I've run into a few.''

''Bunch Karnes isn't the smartest man on earth, but he's hard. Minute you step out into that hall, he'll put a bullet in you.''

''What difference would that make to you?''

''Blood leaves a dark stain on the floor. It's hard to get out.''

''I'll try not to cause you no extra work.'' Dundee moved to the deep, narrow window. Its frame was set so that the window moved sluggishly to one side. He didn't know that he trusted the woman to keep quiet, but circumstances didn't permit him much choice. He slipped out the window and eased to the ground.

Pistol in hand, Dundee edged up to the one side window of the saloon and peered cautiously with one eye. The bartender saw him but gave no sign. Bunch Karnes sat facing the double doors, pistol lying in front of him on a small square table.

Dundee moved hurriedly past the window and on to the front of the building. He still held the pistol, but in a fight, the carbine would suit him better. He walked up to the bay at the hitching rail, drew the carbine and dropped his pistol back into its holster. He moved quietly up to the door. Inside, he could see Karnes seated, back turned, his attention still fixed on the double doors. The bartender saw Dundee and dropped out of sight behind the bar.

Dundee leveled the carbine. ''Karnes, back away from that table. And leave your six-shooter right where it's at.''

Karnes went stiff. Dundee said: ''I got a gun pointed at you. Give me a reason and I'll blow a hole in you they could run a wagon through.''

Karnes slowly stood up. Dundee held his breath, watching the pistol. Karnes' hand was only inches from it. He drew clear of the table and turned, hands empty, face raging.

Dundee said: ''Why don't you just quit? I got no wish to kill you.''

"But I'm going to kill *you,* cowboy."

"Your brother's alive. Why don't you just let it go at that?"

He wasn't reaching Bunch Karnes and knew it. *I ought to shoot him where he stands,* Dundee thought. *That would be the end of it. There won't be an end to it till I do.*

The man was a thief, and in all likelihood a killer. The world would shed few tears if Dundee cut him down. In fact, it would be a better place. But Dundee knew he couldn't pull the trigger, not this way.

"Step away from that table, and leave the pistol."

"I can get another pistol."

A voice in Dundee kept telling him, *Go on and kill him.*

Boots clomped on the front steps. Dundee stepped backward toward the corner, not letting the carbine waver from Karnes.

A big man blocked off most of the light from the doorway, the same heavy-built old man who had been at McCown's.

This was Blue Roan.

Roan Hardesty paused in the door, as if undecided whether to come in or to step back out into the street. He saw then that Karnes was out of reach of his pistol. He cast a long look at Dundee. "You again. They told me some stranger had brung Jayce Karnes to town with a bullethole in him. I ought to've knowed it'd turn out to be you."

Dundee said, "If you got any influence over this man, you better use it."

Hardesty turned to Karnes. "Well?"

"It was him that shot Jayce. I'm fixing to kill him."

"With your six-shooter lying over there on the table? You're just fixing to get your light blowed out, is all. This cowboy looks like he means business, Bunch."

"So do I."

"I need you alive, Bunch. Anyway, the weather's too hot for a funeral. You git yourself along."

"But I . . ."

"I said git on along. I'll talk to you later."

Karnes stared resentfully at Roan Hardesty, his eyes then

drifting to Dundee and spilling their hatred. "I'm going because Roan says to. But don't think it's over, cowboy. I ain't even started yet."

He stomped to the door, down the steps and out into the street, leaving the pistol on the table. Dundee held the carbine, not pointing it directly at Hardesty but not letting the muzzle drop far, either.

Hardesty's voice was deep and gravelly. "You can put away the hardware. I ain't going to do you no harm."

"You can bet your life you're not."

"I promise you. I don't ever break a promise." He turned. "Who the hell is tending bar around here? Where's Cricket?"

The little bartender's head tentatively rose from behind the pine bar, eyes cautiously appraising the situation before he stood up to full height.

Hardesty said, "Whisky, Cricket." He started toward the few small tables. Dundee picked up Karnes' pistol and shoved it into his waistband. Hardesty pulled out a chair. "Set yourself down."

Dundee sat in a corner, where nobody could come up behind him. He watched Hardesty with distrust. The bartender set down a bottle and two glasses. Hardesty pulled the cork and poured the glasses full. "Here's to all the bold and foolish men. And there's a hell of a lot of them." He downed his drink in one swallow. Dundee didn't touch his own. Hardesty noticed. "You don't trust me?"

"I make it a practice not to trust nobody."

"A safe policy. But I gave a promise. Old Blue Roan has broke most of the laws that was ever passed, but he don't break a promise."

Dundee looked at the blue spots on the old man's broad face. "I didn't figure they called you that where you could hear it."

"I'm not ashamed of my face, boy. I bear it like a medal, a thing to be proud of. I got it in the line of duty. I was in the late war, boy, the war between the states. We charged into an artillery emplacement, and the whole thing went up . . . right in my face. I was lucky I kept my eyes. When it was over, I had these marks for life. Sure, I fretted over them awhile, but bye and bye it come to me that they was honest marks. They was like a medal that a man wears all the time and don't even take off with his clothes. They tell the world that Roan Hardesty done his job." He paused to take another drink. "People has said some hard things about me, but there's one thing they can't take away. I done my duty, and I got the marks to prove it." He refilled his glass. "Anyway, I didn't come here to talk about me. I want to find out about *you*. How come you to shoot Jason Karnes?"

"I come up on him and his partner venting the brands on some cattle. He shot at me first."

"Where was this?"

"Back up in the hills, close to a cabin." Dundee pointed his chin.

"How come you fooling around up there, anyway?"

Dundee figured he'd just as well tell it all. "To see what I could find out."

"What *did* you find out?"

"Where some of John Titus' cattle been going."

Roan Hardesty got up from the table. Dundee took a firm grip on the saddlegun. Hardesty walked to the door and looked out at Dundee's horses. "I'm getting old, I guess. Never even noticed the brand on that packhorse when I come in. You working for John Titus?"

Dundee nodded.

Hardesty spat on the floor. "What's old John figure on doing?"

"If I told you that, you'd know as much as *I* do."

Hardesty sat down again, taking another sip out of the glass. "Old Honest John. Bet he never told you he was a pretty good hand with a long rope once. As good a thief as *I* was, pretty near. But he got to letting his conscience talk to him. And then he went and married. Church-going kind, she was. She ruint him; he went honest. Got rich and turned his back on all his old friends."

"Maybe you ought to've done the same."

"No need to. I always had women. Never had to marry one."

"I mean, you should've turned honest."

"The meanest, dullest, most miserable people I know are honest. I like it better where I'm at."

"Somebody may kill you one of these days."

"You, maybe?"

"I hope not." Dundee wouldn't have admitted it, but he found himself drawn to this old reprobate. The old man had the same disarming frankness as John Titus.

"I'd as soon not have to shoot you neither, Dundee. I always had a soft spot for an honest man with guts. Wisht I'd had you with me in the war. A few more like me and you, we'd of whipped them Yankees."

"We might have."

Blue Roan stared at him through narrowed eyes, appraising him like he would judge a horse. "Dundee, I know John Titus. Whatever he's paying you, it ain't enough for the risk. Join up with me and I'll show you where the money's at."

"Venting other people's brands? I reckon not."

"Look at it this way: it's free range, most of it. Biggest part of the land John Titus uses still belongs to the state of Texas. He's taking the use of it free, not paying a dime. And who is the state of Texas? Why, it's me and you and everybody else. John Titus is robbing all us taxpayers. If we run off a few piddling head now and then, it's just our way of making sure he pays something for the grass. We're doing the state of Texas a service, you might say."

The reasoning brought Dundee a smile. He wondered if Roan Hardesty had ever actually paid a dollar of tax to the state of Texas. "I made John Titus a promise. I'll keep it."

The outlaw regretfully accepted Dundee's judgment. "I like a man who keeps a promise. But I can't guarantee you your safety. I can't be responsible for people like Bunch Karnes who think slow but shoot fast."

"I've always took care of myself."

"Keep on doing it. I'd sooner not have you on my conscience." Hardesty stood up to leave, then turned again. "What connection you got with the McCowns?"

"Like I told you, I stopped there and they fed me."

"That's all?"

Worry started building in Dundee. He hadn't intended to

get the McCowns any deeper in trouble than they already were. "That's all, and I'll swear to it. I never saw them before."

Hardesty paused in the doorway. "You're worried because you think this is going to cause me to bear down on them. Don't fret yourself. Them and me, we had our trouble before you ever come here." A faint smile tugged at his big mouth. "That girl is the one you're really thinking about, ain't she? You know, she reminds me of the one old John Titus married. Pass her by, Dundee. She's not for you, all that honeysuckle and home cooking. She'd hogtie you like a slick-eared yearling."

When the old man was gone, Katy Long came back. "I heard most of that. You really come from John Titus?"

"Yep."

"And you tell anybody who asks you?"

"I never been one to lie."

"There's a time and a place for everything. In your place, I'd lie."

"Way I heard it, a couple of other fellers come into this country and lied. They got killed. Me, I just come to find out who's been taking John Titus' cattle, and where they're going with them, that's all. Maybe you'd like to tell me, and save me some trouble."

"You're *already* in trouble. I'm keeping clear of it."

Through the front door Dundee could see the corner of a small mercantile building across the rutted road that passed for a street. He saw a shadow move. He stood up, the carbine in his hands.

Katy Long caught the tension. "What is it?"

"You said you didn't want no trouble. Just stay put." Keeping within the darkness of the room, he moved to a point where he had a better view of the mercantile. He watched a few minutes, waiting for more movement. He saw a hatbrim edge out, and then part of Bunch Karnes' face as the tall man peeked around the corner. He saw a little of a gunbarrel.

Well, Dundee thought regretfully, *I tried. I could as well have shot him awhile ago.*

He maneuvered toward the door, staying close to the

wall. He paused a moment, his shoulder to the wall, gauging where the horses were tied. He didn't want a stray shot to kill his bay or the pack animal. He glanced at the wide-eyed bartender, at the silent woman. He took a deep breath, leaped out the door and lit running.

He took Karnes by surprise. Dundee made three long strides before Karnes stepped out into the open, the pistol extended almost to arm's length in front of him, swinging to try to bring it in line with the running target. Dundee threw himself to the ground. He saw the flash as he brought the carbine up. He aimed at Karnes' chest and squeezed the trigger.

Karnes was flung back grabbing at his shirt in open-mouthed bewilderment, the pistol falling from his hand. He crumpled in a heap.

Cautiously Dundee moved forward, trying to watch Karnes and at the same time looking up and down the street for trouble. He kicked the pistol away, then knelt. He touched Karnes and drew his hand back. Karnes shuddered once, they lay still.

Dundee arose, turned and walked back to the saloon, the carbine smoking in his hands. In the front door stood Katy Long and the little bartender.

A bitter taste in his mouth, Dundee said, "Well, at least we didn't leak blood on your floor."

She didn't back away from him. "Don't take it out on me. When you came here for John Titus, you knew you might kill somebody, or maybe get killed yourself."

He nodded darkly, watching a small crowd begin to gather around the body.

"Then don't blame me. All I do is operate a saloon."

"In an outlaw town."

"Look, cowboy, nobody's taken care of me since I was fourteen. I've minded my own business and left everybody else's alone. I just sell whisky. And you're shooting my customers."

From down the hall Jason Karnes' voice called weakly: "What's happened out there? Somebody tell me what's happened!" In a moment, when no one went to him, he shouted again, anxiety rising: "Bunch! Bunch! Where you at, Bunch? What's happened out there? Bunch!"

Katy Long's handsome face twisted with regret. "I suppose now it's up to me to tell him. Cowboy, I wish to hell you'd ride out of here."

"I was just fixing to leave."

V

Dundee had had a bellyful of Runaway. The hour or so he had whiled away in its contentious clime would do him till hell froze over. As far as he was concerned, they could burn the place to the ground. He even studied a bit about dropping a match in the dry grass, but the wind was blowing in the wrong direction.

Bunch Karnes' blood drying in the sand was not the first Dundee had ever seen, or even the first he'd ever spilled. But this was one experience not improved by repetition. It was a thing that curdled a man's stomach, made him want to get off someplace and face up to his own private demons alone, with no eyes watching. Dundee couldn't see that it would benefit his mission any to hang around Runaway. Chances were somebody would just crowd him into smoking up the carbine again. Let John Titus do the shooting, he thought. They were *his* cattle.

So, looking over his shoulder to be sure the only thing behind him was his shadow, he left Runaway. He rode west awhile, then south. Long days stretched into weeks while he prowled the endless hills, leading the packhorse, looking, mapping, noting brands. Sometimes when he found a cabin or a camp, he would sit among the cedars on some high vantage point and watch for hours with that spyglass, until he was sure he knew what brand went with what people, and whether it was a bonafide brand or some optimistic conversion.

Times, he knew he was not only watching but being watched. Times he would look back and see a horseman or two patiently trailing after him, keeping distance. When he stopped, they stopped. When he rode, they rode.

Nobody made a threatening move, but no longer did he enjoy that feeling of obscurity he had had before the trip to Runaway. He was sure the word about him had spread through all these hills. Maybe they didn't know exactly what he was up to, but they knew he was here. He had to watch for more than cattle now. He took to eating his supper before dark, then riding into the darkness before making cold camp in a thicket somewhere. If they caught him in his blankets, they had to be doing a good job of hunting.

The list of blotted brands kept growing in his tallybook. It had worried him at first because he had so few names to go with the brands. He had no one to go to, no one to ask. But in time he quit stewing about it. He knew the greasy-sack spreads where these brands were claimed. He knew many of the men by appearance, even if he didn't know their names. Besides, most of them probably weren't using the names their mothers had given them anyway. A cowthief by any name was still a cowthief.

There came a point, south, where Dundee found no more T Bar cattle. He came across other fresh brands on grown cattle, and he didn't doubt they'd originally been something else, but not the T Bar. These likely had been rustled in the south and brought north, just as Titus cattle had been stolen in the north and brought south. The way Dundee pictured it, these Llano hills were kind of a crossroads for livestock that had made a nocturnal change in ownership. Some of the cattle he saw here bore all the trademarks of Mexico. They had, no doubt, crossed the Rio Grande in a right smart of a rush.

Well, they were a problem for *somebody,* but not for Dundee. His wages were being paid by John Titus. He began bearing east again, and some to the north. Slowly he was completing a wide circle, and with it, his map. The circle would be closed when he returned to the part of the country where he had started, the Rocker M.

That ranch had been stirring in his mind like a restless squirrel worrying a pile of leaves. Every time he came across a valley which in any way resembled the McCown country, he remembered the young woman standing in the dog-run between the two sections of the sturdy log cabin, her long brown hair floating gently in the wind. He remembered the slenderness of her, the voice, the eyes, the soft woman smell.

She came to him in the golden sunlight of morning, and in the dark of night. She came like a song that has been once heard, and not clearly, but which echoes on and on in memory.

Sometimes, staring at the darkness in a liveoak motte or cedar thicket, he would rub his scratchy beard, smell the dry dust and the smoke that had sifted into the fiber of all his clothes and clung there. He was glad she could not see him this way. He would try to be sure that she never saw him like that again.

He was carrying close to two hundred dollars now, about as much money as he had ever owned at one time in his life. That wasn't much prospect to offer a woman. Times, when he thought of her, he also thought of the free-wheeling, easy-drifting life he'd led, and wondered if he was really ready to change. Damn, but it had been fun. Hard, hungry, stifling hot or freezing cold . . . but fun, just the same. A restlessness still stirred in him, a prickly feeling that came over him every so often and set him to moving without direction, without any purpose except simply to *go*. It wasn't much recommendation to present to a woman. Not *that* kind of woman.

Times, too, he got to wondering if word had drifted back to her about the shooting in Runaway. It probably had. When she next looked at him, would she see Dundee, or would she just see the blood on his hands?

This was mostly a cattle country, but now and again he would run across a band of sheep, usually but not always herded by a Mexican. One sheep outfit he watched was made up of three bands, each band totaling twelve or fifteen hundred sheep.

These, Dundee figured, he didn't have to worry about. A man with a flock of sheep on his hands was too busy to be stealing cows. Maybe more sheep was what it would take to civilize this country.

He was nearing the close-up point on his circle when the heavy rain came. It poured bountifully from a leaden sky, the thunder rolling, the water singing as it filtered down through the hillside grass in a growing flood. Dundee had no idea where to find a ranchhouse. He searched for an overhang he could squeeze under, but he couldn't find one. He huddled beneath the liveoaks until the rain trickled down through the leaves and reached him. The horses hung their heads and took it, for they had never known a roof. But Dundee was soaked to the skin and shivering, his shoulders hunched and his teeth clicking. He decided he had as well be miserable on the move as miserable hunkered on the ground beneath these leaky trees.

At length he came down off of a hill and saw a picket shack. It was a miserable hovel, and any other time he wouldn't have given it a second glance. But now with the rain and the wind chilling him to the bone, it looked as pretty as a marble church. In a set of brush pens he saw goats hunched against the cold. They weren't leggy and spotted and made up of all colors like the Mexican goats he had often seen. These were Angoras, carrying fine, long white mohair which tended to curl into ringlets, even wet. But he was too cold to wonder much or pause to admire a penful of drenched goats. He shouted, "Hello the house!"

A slump-shouldered old man stood in the open door, the wind whipping his snowy beard as he squinted through the rain. He pointed a long, bony finger. "Shed's yonderway. Put your horses up and git yourself back here to the dry."

The shed was mostly just an arbor closed on three sides and given a liberal cover of sod and brush on top to turn the water. He took off saddle and pack and turned the horses loose. He stood a moment under the shed, the first time in hours the rain hadn't been beating down on his back. It felt good here. But the shack would feel even better, for he could see smoke curling up from a stone chimney.

He stopped abruptly as he saw a cowhide stretched across the top of a fence. It was fresh, maybe two or three days old. He started to pass it by, but curiosity was stronger than the cold. The flesh side was turned up, the brand easily visible through it.

The T Bar.

Hell of a country, he thought, where even a goatherder steals cattle.

He dug the pistol out of his saddlebag and strapped it around his waist, beneath his yellow slicker. He stalked across the yard and into the cabin. The old man stared at him with pale gray eyes that were almost lost beneath bushy gray brows. A Mexican boy of eighteen or so sat on a wooden-framed goathide cot in a corner, rolling a brown-paper cigarette.

Dundee was too cold to play games. He flung the challenge. "You got a cowhide out yonder with a T Bar on it!"

The old man nodded as if it wasn't any news to him. "I bet you're that feller I been hearing about. Ain't your name *Dandy?*"

"It's *Dun*dee. And I asked you about that hide."

The old man looked sympathetic. "You're cold. And I bet you ain't yet et."

"I'm asking you for an answer."

"I bet you're hungry. Well, you peel some of them wet clothes off and we'll have dinner here directly. You'll feel like a new man when you've surrounded some of this fresh beef."

"About that hide. . . ."

"Let's don't talk business right now. You're cold and hungry, and I never did like to argue with a hungry man. A man just ain't reasonable. You git your belly filled, then we'll talk."

A Dutch oven sat astraddle some blazing oakwood in the open fireplace, steak sizzling. Dundee pointed his chin. "That steak yonder, I reckon it came out from under that hide?"

The old fellow nodded.

Dundee exclaimed: "That's T Bar beef. You expect me to eat it?"

"Why not? You work for old Titus, don't you? And if you was on the home ranch you'd be eating Titus beef, wouldn't you? So what's the difference if you eat it *here?* Who's better entitled to it?"

The off-center logic went by Dundee so fast he couldn't argue with it. The steak smelled good. And the old man had called the tune: Dundee was hungry as a she-wolf with six pups.

The Mexican wasn't saying anything. Dundee didn't know if he understood English, even. But the herder sat like a suspicious watchdog, glancing protectively at the old man, most of the time keeping his narrowed eyes fastened on Dundee. Dundee had a cold feeling that if he made any menacing move toward the old goat man, he'd have to beat that young Mexican to the floor or be crushed himself. In addition, there was a black and white dog of a breed or mixture that Dundee didn't know. It sat under the Mexican's feet, gaze never wavering from the stranger. Dundee might have to fight *him,* too.

Coffee boiled in a pot in the corner of the fireplace. The old man poured a cup of cold water in to settle the grounds and brought the pot up to set it on the rough table. It left black ash marks, but they were hardly noticeable; the table was already as discolored as it could get. "Steak's done. Got a pot of beans, too. Hope you don't mind cold bread."

The tinware was battered and tarnished, but that was of no matter. The food was good. Dundee's eyebrows went up when the old man lifted one piece of steak out of the popping grease and dropped it into an old tin plate on the dirt floor, for the dog. The dog sniffed it eagerly but knew enough to wait for it to cool. The old man dropped him a couple of cold biscuits to keep him busy. "Man's got a good working dog, he's got to take care of him," he said.

Dundee wondered how John Titus would appreciate it, seeing his beef fed to a goatherder's dog.

The meal over, Dundee leaned back and rubbed his stomach. "That was sure fine."

The old man took the compliment with grace. "No trick to it if you got good beef."

"Such as Titus beef?"

"I tried not to notice the brand." The old man smiled gently. "While ago I said you'd be eating T Bar beef if you was on the home ranch. Fact is, I bet you'd be eating some neighbor's. John Titus kills strays, just like everybody else. A man's own beef don't ever taste as good."

"Titus might not see it your way."

"The fact is, Dandy, I kept that steer from being stole."

"What do you mean?"

"Some fellers brought a herd of cattle through here three . . . four days ago, heading south. They scattered my goats by accident, so to make it right they offered me this steer. He was lame and couldn't keep up anyway."

"The rest of the cattle . . . they carry a T Bar brand?"

"Like I said, in this country I don't ever see no brands."

"The men driving those cattle . . . who were they?"

The oldtimer smiled thinly. "Now, Dandy, the way I lived to get so old was by not seeing anything that wasn't my business, and not saying nothing about what I didn't see."

"I could tell John Titus you been eating his beef."

"If you think it'll make things right, I'll swap you for that steer. He was lame and not worth much. I'll pick out two of my top goats, and you can take them along."

"What would I do with two goats?"

"That'd be up to you. All I want is to pay a debt if I got one. And I ain't sure as I do. After all, I *did* save that steer from being stole."

Dundee shrugged. He didn't figure John Titus would be very hard on a man who just butchered a steer once in a while to eat. Especially if Dundee never told him. Dundee changed the subject. "Them are unusual-looking goats you got. They work good in this country?"

"Them is Angorys . . . *hair*-goats. You shear mohair off of them, like you shear wool off of a sheep. They're the coming thing for this part of the country, once the cowthieves leave. They eat brush and stuff like that. If he has to, a goat can live on next to nothing. And a man can live on goat. Hard to starve a goat man to death.''

The old man stared through the door at the rain still pelting down. ''Looks like it's liable to hang on awhile. You're welcome to stay here, Dandy.''

''Much obliged.''

''Where you headed when it's over with? You figuring on trying to trail them cattle?''

Dundee shook his head. ''Won't be no tracks left after this rain. No, I reckon I'll go see some folks. Then I'll head back to the T Bar.''

''This is a good country down here. You could do worse than stay.''

''What for? I got no cattle, and I don't aim to steal any.''

''You could start small and build as the country builds.''

''This is nothing but an outlaw country.''

''The outlaws won't last. They're just part of a country's growing up, like a kid has to put up with measles and chickenpox. One day they'll all be gone, but the country'll be here. All we need in these hills is some good people . . . and a little more rain.''

''That,'' said Dundee, ''is all *hell* needs.''

VI

Dundee had jogged along in a deliberate trot all day, keeping a checkrein on his patience. Now the double log cabin lay ahead of him, and patience evaporated like a summer mist. He touched spurs to the bay, picking up into an easy lope.

All morning he had watched for signs of Warren McCown or Uncle Ollie. He thought they might be riding these hills and the long valleys to check their cattle after the rains. Now, approaching the homeplace spring and the corrals, he looked for the men again. He still didn't see them. A single horse stood in the pen, near the saddleshed. Unsaddling his bay and dropping the pack, Dundee noticed that Uncle Ollie's saddle hung on its rack, but Warren's was gone.

The lazy old whelp probably waited till Warren was out of sight, then snuck back to loaf, Dundee thought. He spread dry mesquite beans for the horses, then set out afoot toward the cabin.

Millie stood in the dog-run, smiling, her long hair adrift in the south wind which had come up strong now that the rains were over and the clouds broken away. He walked briskly toward her. She didn't wait; she hurried to meet him halfway. She stopped when they were three paces apart, her eyes ashine. She made an instinctive gesture of opening her arms to receive him, realized what she had done and brought her hands together.

Dundee stopped. He fought a compelling urge to scoop her into his arms. A man didn't do that . . . not to a woman like this. He swallowed and remembered his place. He had no right.

He crushed his hat in his hands the way he wanted to crush *her*.

"Dundee! I don't know when I've ever been so glad to see somebody."

"Been a while, ain't it?" He rubbed his face and managed a nervous smile. "This time I shaved *before* I got here." He had washed out his clothes, too, though they had dried with the wrinkles of wadded-up paper.

"You didn't have to," she said.

"Yes, I had to."

She smiled, and watching her warmed him like a long drink of whisky. He'd never seen a woman before that a man could get drunk just looking at.

She said, "Dundee, I hope you can stay."

"Well. . . ."

"Warren's not here, and Uncle Ollie's had a fall."

"Bad hurt?"

"Doesn't seem like he's got any bones broken. But he's sore and stiff, and it pains him to move. I need help with him till Warren gets back."

He wondered suspiciously whether the old man was really lame or just lazy. "Where did Warren go?"

"Went south to buy cattle."

Dundee stopped walking. "South, you say? Why south?"

She saw the look on his face and stared in puzzlement. "North of us there's nothing much but T Bar. There are already too many T Bar cattle running around here with somebody else's brand on them. Warren didn't want any, not even *with* a bill of sale."

Remembering what the old goat man had told him, Dundee counted back. "How many days since Warren left?"

"Six. Six days and seven hours." There was sadness in the way she said it.

Six. He frowned, counting on his fingers, finally shaking his head. *Not Warren. Surely not Warren.*

"Come on," Millie said, "let me take you to Uncle Ollie. He'll be real tickled to see a friendly face."

If I find the old codger faking, it ain't going to be none too friendly.

Uncle Ollie lay on his cot, atop the old woolen blankets. He had his britches on for propriety, a concession to Millie, Dundee guessed. But his faded red underwear was his cover from the waist up. It bore patches that must have been stitched there by Millie McCown's patient fingers. Ollie raised himself up on his left elbow and stuck out his right hand, wincing as if it caused him great pain. "Howdy, Dundee. Millie said she seen you ride in, but I didn't hear you. Used to could hear a grasshopper spit from a hundred yards. Used to do a heap of things I can't do no more."

Dundee asked with suspicion, "Horse throw you off?"

Sheepishly the old man said: "Wisht one had. There's a little bit of glory in that. Truth is, I was fishing and fell off of the bank."

Dundee nodded. It was in character, all right. The

old man was probably spreading it on thicker than it really was, but he was likely telling the truth in the main.

Millie said: "Just the same, we'll tell Warren it was a horse."

Dundee shrugged. "I reckon a little lie once in a while don't hurt nothing, long's it's for a good cause."

Ollie smiled thinly. "Glad you see it my way, Dundee. Wisht Warren did."

I expect he sees more than you think he does, Dundee said to himself.

Ollie complained: "Way he goes all the time, he'll be old before long hisself. Then maybe he'll know. Only it'll be too late then for me. I'll be dead and in the grave." He sat up and dropped his legs off the cot, wincing and groaning. Millie had moved across the room to the cabinet, where she had some biscuit dough working. Ollie whispered, "Help me outside, will you?"

Dundee took a thin arm around his shoulder and assisted the old man to his feet. Ollie moved slowly, sucking breath between his teeth. Outside, he waved for a pause to rest. "Much obliged. Some things a man can't have a woman help him do. Been having to make this trip all by myself, an it's been pure hell."

"Ollie, when did you take this fall?"

"Why, it was the day Warren left. The very same day. How come you to ask?"

"Just curious." Dundee glanced toward the woodpile, knowing Millie had done most of the chopping herself, unless Warren had left her a supply. Likely he hadn't. That's what Ollie was supposed to be for.

Back in the cabin, Ollie stretched on the cot and began to talk about the old days, when the world had been freer and fresher and the air keener and men more honest and life had been a joy to live. Dundee only half listened, nodding when he thought he ought to, agreeing now and again with a quiet "unh-hunh." Mostly he watched Millie McCown kneading dough for supper biscuits, cutting the dough and putting it out in a flat pan. He watched her roll steak in flour and never even wondered what brand was on the hide it came from under.

Uncle Ollie came completely unwound at the supper table, and Dundee noticed that even though the old man's legs were stiff and sore, his jaw swiveled quite easily, both for eating and for talking. Ollie had known every famous cowman from the Rio Grande to the Canadian River, seemed like. He had known every gunfighter and had personally witnessed every gunfight of any notoriety since the fall of the Alamo, and Dundee wondered how come he had missed that one.

Millie finished washing the dishes, put away the wet drying towel, looked at Dundee a moment, then walked to the door. "It's nice out tonight. I think I'll get some air," she said.

Ollie leaned on his elbow, nursing his pipe, eyes focused on something far beyond the room, far back in time. "Them was the days, Dundee. I tell you, it ain't nothing like that no more. People don't enjoy theirselves the way they used to."

Dundee looked outside at Millie. "Maybe they do. Maybe it's just a new bunch doing it now."

Ollie clicked his pipe against his teeth, listening to no one but himself. "No, sir, it ain't the same. I mind the time—before the war, it was—me and my brother was out on the Keechi. . . ." The old man talked on, immersed in his story-telling, his mind lost in ancient memories . . . or maybe it was ancient dreams . . . it would be hard to separate one from the other. Dundee eased out the door and left him there, still talking to himself.

Millie leaned against one of the heavy cedar posts that held up the brush arbor. She stared down the valley into the gathering dusk. Dundee knew she heard him, but she didn't look around. She said: "Expecting Warren back any day now. He's been gone an awfully long time."

"Just six days, you said. Give him time. Cattle move slow."

"So do the hours, when you're out here so far from anybody, just by yourself. Oh, I don't mean that Warren and Uncle Ollie aren't good company. But I mean, you go so terribly long here sometimes and never see a soul except family. Then, when even one of the family leaves for awhile, it's like somebody had died.''

''This isn't good for a woman. You shouldn't be out here.''

''I belong. It's the only real home I ever had. When Dad was living, we just drifted around from ranch to ranch. Never owned anything, never stayed anywhere long enough to gather from the gardens we planted, even. Warren said we were gypsies, always on the move, never leaving anything behind us but wagon tracks. He said someday he was going to find him a place and put down roots so deep they couldn't be pulled up by anything or anybody. And I guess this is the place.''

''For a woman, it ain't much.''

''It's home. When you've wandered most of your life, it means something to stand on a piece of ground and call it your own. It gives you a feeling . . . I couldn't tell you what it's like . . . to look across that valley yonder and know it's yours . . . to know that come tomorrow you'll still be here . . . and next month . . . and next year.''

''It's lonesome, just the same.''

''Nothing is ever perfect. This is a lot better than we *used* to have. And it'll be even better yet. Warren will see to that.''

Warren. Dundee realized that her brother had taken on the aspect of a father to her. The sun rose and set with Warren McCown, and would, until some other man came along to establish a new and different relationship that would displace him.

He said: ''You won't always depend on Warren. One of these days some cowboy will take a good look at you and carry you off.''

She turned, and he saw in her eyes a want so deep that it startled him. She said: ''He wouldn't have to go anywhere. He could stay right here.''

Dundee looked away, somehow off balance. ''Maybe, if he was thataway inclined.''

''This is a good place. A man could be happy here.''

"If he was the right kind of a man for it . . . if his feet didn't keep getting the itch to move on."

"If a man found what he was looking for, he wouldn't *want* to move anymore, would he?"

"Some of us never know what we're looking for. We're just looking."

"When you do find it, do you think you'll know?"

"I couldn't rightly say. I ain't found it so far."

She took in a slow breath. "You could have, without realizing."

Dundee looked away, fishing a small sack out of his pocket and rolling himself a cigarette, spilling most of the tobacco. He stole a glance and found her frowning in thought. Finally she asked: "Why do you work for John Titus?"

"For money, I guess."

"You could as easy work for somebody else."

"He's paid me good, and there's more coming. For once in my life I'm going to have me a stake to show for my time."

"And when you get that money, what'll you do with it?"

"Been studying about that a right smart. I'd like to have more to show for the next thirty years than I've had for the last thirty. Been thinking I might set me up a business."

"Like what?"

"Oh, like maybe a saloon. An honest one, of course."

Her eyes disapproved. "A saloon?"

"Beats cowboying. One time I spent three hard months on a ranch. Never saw the bunkhouse in daylight the whole time. Worked till I didn't even sweat anymore; just oozed blood. Went to town finally, and in three days I spent every cent I'd made in three months. *He* didn't sweat. Heaviest thing he lifted in the whole three days was my money as he toted it to the bank."

"Dundee, don't you want something better in life than a saloon?"

"It's a good investment. When times are easy, everybody spends free. Times get hard, they drink to forget their troubles. Either way, the saloonkeeper walks a-jingling."

"There's more to life than money."

"That's what they say, but I never seen much evidence of it."

"There's more to you than you let on, Dundee. You could set your sights higher than that ... a lot higher."

"What do you figure I ought to aim at?"

"You could take your money and buy cattle with it. Maybe there wouldn't be many at first, but they'd be *yours*. You could take that little start and build, the way Warren does. You wouldn't have to work for other people. You'd have cattle of your own, something that belonged to you and you could be proud of."

"It's hard work punching cows. I *know*."

"When the cows belong to you, it's not like working for the other man."

Dundee figured he was listening to a lecture from Warren McCown, second-handed. "Sure, I've thought about that. But there's something always worried me. What if I got myself all set on a place and had my roots down too deep to pull them up, and then my feet commenced itching again? What if I came to hate the sight of the place? What if it turned out to be more of a jail than a promised land?"

She touched his hand. Her fingertips were warm and startling. It was as if he had brushed his hand against a wire fence in a lightning storm. She said, "Maybe you wouldn't ever get to feeling that way ... if you had somebody with you. . . ."

He found his lips dry. He licked them with a quick, furtive touch of his tongue. "Millie, I might even get tired of her, too. Then she'd be miserable, and so would I." Her fingers tightened on his hand. He felt heat rising in his blood, and he drew his hand away. "Millie, some men it's best to leave alone. There's a right smart you don't know."

"But there's a lot I *do* know. You're a brave man, and you're kind."

"Kind? Maybe you ain't heard. I shot a man in Runaway."

Her lips tightened. "I heard. Somebody told Warren."

"That ought to be enough to change your mind about me."

"You didn't *want* to shoot him, did you?"

He shook his head. "But I did do it, and that's what counts."

"It doesn't count. You just did what came necessary. I don't imagine it's an easy thing to live with." Her eyes softened in sympathy. "I've heard that when a man has to kill, it haunts him, that the dead man won't let him rest."

"I've lost some sleep, all right, but it's been mostly from worrying about his live friends."

Millie laced her fingers together and squeezed them. She tried to look at him but cut her glance away when their gaze met. Dundee stared at her with hungry eyes, his pulse quickening, his hands shaking a little. He could sense a silent call reaching out to him, a cry of loneliness she didn't know how to express.

And there was a want in *him*, too, deep as a canyon. It was that want which had brought him back here.

Hoarsely she said, "Dundee, I don't think I ever knew a man quite like you."

He had been about to reach for her, to grasp her arms and pull her to him. Now her words fell on him like a sudden dash of cold water. She'd never really known *any* man, he was sure. She waited, trembling in expectation of something she didn't even understand. She was untouched, unprepared.

Times, he'd thought how pleasant it would be to walk into a situation like this, like stumbling across an unclaimed gold mine where all you had to do was reach and take.

Now he drew away, suddenly grave. "Millie, go in the house."

"What . . . ?"

Sternly he said: "You better go see after Uncle Ollie. He may be needing something."

He sensed the disappointment that folded in around her like a dark cloud. "Did I do something wrong?"

"No, but if you stay out here, *I* might."

Face coloring, she spoke almost in a whisper: "I don't guess you'd do anything I didn't want you to."

"There'd come a time you'd wish I hadn't. You'd hate

me then, and likely I'd have a contempt for myself. You got a lot to learn yet, Millie. I don't want it on my conscience that I was the one taught you.''

VII

Although Uncle Ollie lapped up sympathy like an old dog takes to gravy, Dundee decided it wasn't all put-on with him. The fall had really hurt the old man, and at his age repairs came slow and painfully. Dundee wanted to stay, and warm himself in the glow that came upon him whenever Millie was close. But times, the temptation to reach out and take her was almost more than he could push aside. He found that he feared himself more than he had ever feared any man.

He would have left had it not been for Uncle Ollie. The old man would be a burden to the girl if she had to take care of him alone. Dundee chewed and fretted. Once he made up his mind to leave and went so far as to catch his horses. Then he went in from the woodpile with a fresh-cut armload of stovewood and saw Millie struggling to help her hungry uncle to the table. Dundee knew he had to stay till Warren got home. But he wouldn't stay an hour longer than that. Millie being the way she was, it was just too damned dangerous.

He purposely spent most of his time away from the house, chopping enough wood to carry halfway through next winter, stacking rocks for Warren's stone corrals, hoeing weeds out of the garden patch, anything to keep him mind-changing distance from temptation. Being close to her all the time—studying about her so much—kept him fighting against himself.

Maybe what he ought to do was slip off for a quick, quiet little ride into Runaway, where he might find a bit of diversion down toward the end of the street.

Uncle Ollie was aware, too. Once when Dundee helped him take a walk out back, Ollie said, "Millie's kind of hit you between the eyes, ain't she?"

"What do you mean by that?"

"I been noticing the way you watch her. If I was of a violent nature, being her uncle and all, I could shoot you for the things you been thinking."

Dundee's face went warm. "You got an awful imagination."

"I see what I see." Ollie's eyes narrowed with a hint of craftiness. "You know, Dundee, half of everything here belongs to her. If you was to marry her, you'd have as much to say around here as Warren does."

Dundee held his silence, knowing Ollie was fishing.

Ollie continued: "Warren expects too much out of an old man. He's working me into my grave, I tell you. But you, Dundee, you could put a stop to that. You got a feeling for an old man."

"You're a dirty-minded, shameless schemer."

"And old man has got to scheme. He can't fight."

Dundee was wondering how much longer he would be able to stand it here when he saw the spring wagon laboring its way up the valley, the team straining in the afternoon sun, bouncing the wagon across the ford and up out of the streambed. Dundee dropped a heavy rock he had been about to place on the fence. He straightened his aching shoulders and squinted. Warren? *He* was supposed to come in with a herd of cattle. In any case, Warren hadn't taken the McCown wagon with him. It stood by the saddleshed. Dundee dusted his hands on his trousers, wiped sweat from his face onto his sleeve and started toward the house, watching the wagon.

He could make out two horses being led behind it, and two people sitting on the seat. One was a woman.

"Millie," he called, "you got company coming."

Millie stepped out of the house, wiping flour from her

hands onto an apron, lifting one hand to shade her eyes. ''I can't make them out.''

Dundee stepped into the house and came back with a pistol strapped on his hip. He said, ''The man is Roan Hardesty.''

Blue Roan slouched on the wagonseat like a huge sack of oats, the reins in his big hands. Beside him, the saloon woman Katy Long sat with her back straight as a ramrod. If he hadn't known better, Dundee might have mistaken her for a schoolteacher.

Bet she could teach me some things, though, he thought. *Katy Long. Bet that ain't her real name. Bet she ain't used her right name in so long she'd have to study to remember what it is.*

Roan wheeled the wagon into the yard. Dundee saw two men in the back of it, one sitting up, one lying atop a stack of blankets. His gaze fell first upon the bandage. He remembered John Titus' contrary boy, the one he'd had that scrap with in Titusville.

This was Son Titus!

The old renegade reined the team to a stop. He took a careful look around, like a coyote surveying a chickenhouse, then tipped his shapeless hat to the girl by the arbor. ''Evening, Miss Warren.'' He shifted his gaze to Dundee, and his eyes seemed to laugh. ''Howdy, Dundee. Figured this was where I'd find you at. I got me a couple of problems here I want to dump in your lap.''

Dundee glanced at the woman. Katy Long wasn't looking at him; she was staring at Millie McCown.

Dundee walked up to the wagonbed and peered into one defiant eye of the Titus heir. The other eye was swollen shut. ''Son Titus, what the hell do you think you're doing here?'' Dundee said.

''I come a-hunting cowthieves. I come to do the job *you* was hired for.''

Roan Hardesty shifted his great bulk in the wagonseat to look back. ''He's the old bear's cub, all right; ain't no doubt about that. Got the looks of old John, and the temper. I *would* say he lacks the brains. Must've took after some other branch of the family.''

A bunch of questions were rattling around in Dundee's head, but he figured he'd get them all answered in due course if he would keep his mouth shut.

Roan siad: "He come into Runaway proud and loud. Except for a couple of saloon girls, he didn't make no friends."

Dundee asked, "What did you do, run a bunch of horses over him?"

The old thief shook his head. "Soon's I got the word who he was, I give an order: nobody was to kill him. Guess I ought to've said nobody was supposed to *hurt* him, because they tried to see how far they could go *without* killing him." He glanced down at the sullen Son Titus. "He asked for it. Felt kind of like stomping him a little myself, but I always been too good-natured for that kind of thing."

Dundee snorted to himself. *I'll bet.* He looked at the cowboy who lay on the blankets. "Who is this?"

Roan replied regretfully: "Compadre of young Titus. He done what he could to get the boy out of trouble. He's got a bullet in his shoulder. Or *did* have. Katy took it out."

Dundee glanced at the saloon woman. "Playing nurse again. Maybe you missed your calling."

Her eyes flashed. "What makes you think you know what my calling *is?*"

Old Roan growled: "Now look, I already seen enough fighting to do me awhile. I'm turning these two boys over to you, Dundee."

"Why me?"

"They're T Bar property. I want you to get them back to old John. One more thing: make damn sure this cub don't turn up in Runaway again. Next time I might not be there to protect him. Somebody might put a permanent part in his hair."

Dundee said, "Come on, Son Titus, I'll help you out of the wagon."

Young Titus snapped: "I can get out by myself. Just you move aside and don't get in my way." He scooted his rump down the wagonbed and gingerly eased to the ground, favoring sore muscles and miscellaneous lacerations. "If you want to, though, you can help my friend Tobe. He's not in no shape to help himself.''

Dundee climbed up. Carefully he lifted the cowboy, who sucked air between his teeth but didn't cry out. Katy Long quickly left the wagonseat. "Take it easy with him," she spoke sharply. "He's not a beef to be jerked around."

"I'm handling him gentle as I know how."

"Then you don't know very much." She stood at the rear of the wagon, ready to help bring the cowboy down. Son Titus waited there too, though Dundee figured he would be as much help as a split slicker in a rainstorm. Millie McCown came to stand beside Katy Long. Dundee got one arm under the cowboy's back, the other under his legs, then eased him down to the women. Sensibly, they shouldered Son Titus aside. Dundee said, "Just hold him now till I can get down out of the wagon." He glanced at Millie. "Looks like you got you another invalid."

"It's all right." She had a lot of patience, he thought.

On the ground, Dundee got the cowboy's good arm around his shoulder. Tobe had just enough strength to keep from wilting completely. "Hang on, pardner," Dundee gritted. "We'll get you inside in a minute."

"It's all right," the cowboy rasped.

Old Blue Roan had silently watched from the wagonseat. Now he laboriously climbed off, his weight pulling the wagon down heavily on one side, even turning the wheel a little as he put a foot on a spoke and shifted his bulk to it.

Dundee said, "I'm curious how you knew I'd be here."

Roan smiled. "I got eyes all over these hills. I've knowed pretty much where you been from one day to the next, ever since you rode out of Runaway. I figured once you got *here*, you'd stay awhile. *I* would, was I a mite younger."

Dundee glanced at Millie. She showed no sign that she caught Roan's implication. Katy Long did, though. She gave Dundee a glare that would kill mesquite.

Lying on his cot, Ollie McCown stared in amazement as they brought the cowboy into the room. "What the hell?" He saw Blue Roan then, and he cringed, dread clouding his eyes.

Roan said: "Lay easy, friend. I come here in a flush of generosity."

Millie pointed toward Warren's unused cot. "Put him there. If Warren comes home, he can sleep outside under the arbor, like Dundee."

Roan looked disappointed.

Katy Long stared gravely at the wounded cowboy, then at Millie. "We shouldn't have moved him this far, but Roan was afraid he'd come to harm in town. He needs to heal awhile before he's moved again."

Roan said: "I feel kind of responsible, seeing as some of my boys done this to him. I don't expect you got any too much vittles in the house. I fetched some extra."

Millie straightened in a flash of pride that reminded Dundee of Warren McCown. "We're not hungry. We can afford to feed an extra one or two."

"No offense. Dundee, you want to help me fetch them vittles in."

He phrased it like an order rather than a question. Heading for the door, Dundee heard Katy ask Millie, "You ever dressed a bullet wound before?" Millie hadn't. Katy said, "He needs fresh bandaging now, so I'll show you."

Roan had brought the goods in a couple of canvas sacks. In one were dried beans and fruit and some flour and coffee. In the other, canned goods clanked together as Dundee hoisted the heavy sack to his shoulder. He glanced suspiciously at the old brandburner. "This don't sound like what I've heard about you."

"Them stories was mostly lies."

"Maybe not. I seen you awhile back, trying to run a bluff on the McCowns here."

"It wasn't no bluff."

"Then how come you to bring these groceries?"

The old man scowled. "Not for the McCowns. Not Warren McCown, anyway." He paused, face softening. "I reckon I owe John Titus a little something for old times . . . and for all the T Bar cows that have went into my pockets. I figure it's going to be some days before you can haul that cowboy home. I want to send John his son back well-fed and in one piece . . . give or take a couple of teeth.''

Dundee waited a moment to see if Roan was going to carry the other sack, but it was obvious Roan hadn't really meant for Dundee to *help* him; he had meant for Dundee to tote them all. Dundee carried the groceries in, dropped the sack on the floor and came back for the other. Roan reached under the wagonseat and brought out a couple of six-shooters with the gunbelts wrapped around them.

''Better drop these into that sack. They belong to young Titus and that cowboy. Was I you, I'd keep them hid till you get them boys back to John Titus.'' The blue spots on his face seemed to darken. ''One thing for damn sure: don't you let that Titus button go back to Runaway. Sit on him if you have to, or tie him to a cedar tree. I can't watch all the time.''

''He must've ripped things up a little.''

''He's a brassy little devil; I'll give him that. Rode into town like he was somebody come. Scattered the news that he was thief-hunting, and he wasn't leaving without some scalps. I told the boys to let him alone, so they all just turned their backs on him. Then's when he found the women. I tell you, between loud talk and raw whisky and warm women, he was having hisself a high old time. That cowboy, he done his best to get him out of there, but I reckon young Titus had saved up too much of an appetite. I swear, Dundee, it's a mortal shame how that boy has been deprived.

''He tried to provoke them boys of mine by calling them cowthieves, but they all knew they was anyway, and they had my orders. When the fight finally *did* start, it was over one of the girls. Son got to poaching on private territory. If it hadn't been for the cowboy, Titus would've got killed. The cowboy took the bullet for him. Next time, it might be different. Watch him.''

''I will.''

''And maybe if you're busy watching *him,* you won't be coming back to Runaway yourself, either. You didn't leave no friends there that I noticed.''

''I expect I'll be back.''

"It'd be a pity. I can't help but like a man a little bit when I respect him. I'd hate to shovel dirt in your face."

Through the open door they could see Katy Long gesturing, telling Millie how to take care of the cowboy's wounds. The old outlaw watched, a gleam in his eyes. "I swear, Dundee, that's a good-looking filly, that McCown girl. And unbroke; a man could train her to suit hisself. Was I you, I'd a whole lot rather spend my time playing games with her than stirring up dust over in Runaway."

Dundee frowned but made no reply. Hardesty went on: "An old man ought not to have to give advice to a young man in matters like this, but I will. Opportunity don't knock often in this life. When it does, you better grab."

"You don't know a good woman when you see one."

"A *good* woman is just one that ain't been given the right opportunities."

Katy Long came outside and beckoned silently with a quick jerk of her chin. Her eyes were sharp, her words clipped. "Dundee, I've told the girl what to do, but she's never had any experience with this kind of thing. You may have to help her."

Sensing her distaste, Dundee stiffened in resentment. "I will."

"There's something else you could do to help her, too. You could leave her alone."

"What do you mean by that?"

"I mean the girl is young, and she's green. She's like a wild flower way out on the prairie. She's never met your kind of man before, and she doesn't know how to defend herself."

"Who told you she's had to?"

"I saw the way she looked at you. You've got her eating out of your hand."

Heat rose in Dundee's face. It was bad enough having to answer for the things he *did* do.

She said: "I'm used to gunfighters. I've even gotten accustomed to thieves. But I'll be damned if I can find any excuse for a man who would take advantage of innocence."

"What would *you* know about innocence?"

Her eyes flashed like lightning against a dark sky. "Enough that I respect it when I see it. It's a sad thing when you lose it; I can remember."

In spite of his resentment, Dundee sensed sincerity in this woman. "If it's any satisfaction to you, I ain't touched her."

She stared hard, and he knew it would be difficult to hide a lie from those sharp eyes. Her gaze lost its edge. "I'd like to believe that."

"Take it or leave it. It's the truth."

Her back lost its rigidity. "Don't tell me you haven't been tempted."

"Hell yes, I been tempted. You think I'm made out of wood?"

For a moment he thought she came close to a relieved smile. "Well then, remember this: the test of a man isn't whether he's ever tempted or not. It's whether he resists temptation."

He glanced at the wagon. "It'll be easier now. You've brought two extra pairs of eyes to watch me."

Now she *did* smile, though it was a fleeting thing and touched with malice. "If the temptation gets too strong, there are women in Runaway."

"Including you?"

"My business is whisky."

Roan hollered: "Come on, Katy. It's a long ways back to town."

Dundee suggested to Katy, "If you're worried about Millie, you could stay here and protect her."

Katy shook her head. "I might have to protect myself."

Dundee watched the wagon slowly drop down into the ford and climb out on the far side of the stream. He turned then toward the cabin, bracing himself a little. His eyes found Son Titus as he walked through the door. "You damnfool button, what do you think you was doing in Runaway?"

Defiantly Titus said, "You'd know, if you'd been doing the job my dad hired you for, instead of laying up here passing the time with some nester girl."

Dundee glanced at Millie and saw the color rise. He clenched his fist. "Watch out what you say, boy."

"If you'd been out doing what you was supposed to, you'd of knowed they made a big raid on the T Bar and run off enough cattle to make a whole herd for some greasy-sack outfit like *this* one."

"So you decided to try to make the old man see you've growed up. You decided to go and wipe out the cowthieves all by yourself."

"I ain't finished yet."

"Yes, you are. You've all but got your friend here killed. If it wasn't for old Roan, you'd be laying out yonder someplace now, feeding buzzards."

Son Titus' right eye was dark and swollen, but his left one shone with anger. "You act mighty thick with that splotchy-faced old scoundrel. I've had a notion all along you'd fall in cahoots with that wild bunch."

It was on Dundee's tongue to tell Son Titus that Roan had once been a friend of his father. But anger had a tendency to make words come hard for him. It was easier to ball up a fist and hit something. "Son Titus, if a man just worked at it a little bit, he could get to where he didn't like you atall."

"I got friends enough. I don't need *you*."

Dundee pointed his chin at the cowboy who lay in silence on Warren McCown's cot. "You like to've lost one of them. Till he gets in shape to move, you'll stay here and behave yourself. I'm not going to take any foolishness off of you, Son Titus. Cross me and I'll slap you down."

Titus' open eye glowered. "You're forgetting, Dundee; I don't take orders off of you. You're working for us."

Dundee corrected him. "I'm working for your old daddy. And you *will* take orders or I'll pack you home tied up like a long-eared maverick."

Son's swollen eye and his stiff joints hadn't left him unable to walk. He limped painfully out of the cabin, trying to stomp but hurting too badly to make it effective.

I'll likely have to clean his plow again before he makes up his mind to wear the bridle, Dundee thought. *And I believe I could do it smiling.*

Dundee turned toward the cot where the cowboy lay. "What did they say his name was?"

Millie's hands were clasped nervously, as if she had expected a fight. "Tobe, I think they said."

The cowboy spoke, barely above a whisper. "Yes, it's Tobe. Tobe Crane."

Surprised, Dundee said: "I thought you was out like a dry lamp. By rights you could just as well've been dead. Didn't you have better sense?"

"Son was bound and bedamned. I had to try and help him."

Dundee frowned. "How old are you?"

"Twenty-one."

"If you want to reach twenty-two, you got some things to learn. One of them is to pick better friends. I'd as soon carry dynamite in my hip pocket as to ride with Son Titus."

"Son's all right. He's just trying to show his old daddy . . . to be the old man all over again . . . and he don't know how."

"I hope he lives long enough to learn." Dundee's forehead furrowed. Underneath those bandages and that bruised skin, he thought there was something familiar about the face. "Wasn't you trying to help Son Titus bob my horse's tail in Titusville?"

"We didn't mean you no harm. I'm glad we didn't finish the job."

Dundee turned as if to go. The cowboy weakly lifted his hand. "Dundee, Son has got his faults, but he's got the makings. The old man knows it, but he don't know how to show it. He's afraid of making Son's head swell, I reckon. So he treats Son like a little boy, and Son keeps on trying to prove he's not. That's all that's the matter with him. You got to understand that about Son."

"Does the old man know Son went to Runaway?"

"No. He give Son orders to go north after a string of horses. Far as old John knows, there's where he went."

Dundee glanced at the girl, whose eyes warmed with sympathy as she looked down on the cowboy. "Millie'll take good care of you. Soon's you can stand the trip, I'll take you and Son home."

"That's decent of you, Dundee."

"I'm being paid for it."

Outdoors, he found Son Titus slumped in a rawhide chair beneath the brush arbor. Son gave Dundee a quick look with his good eye and cut his face away. "I ain't in no shape to fight you right now, Dundee. But I'll heal," he said.

VIII

The distant bawling of cattle drifted across the long valley and fell on Dundee's ears as welcome as the jingle of coin to a broke cowpuncher. Warren McCown was back. Dundee saddled his horse and rode south toward the sound, whistling.

Tobe Crane wasn't ready to be moved yet, but Dundee seriously considered taking Son Titus home anyway. He could come back for Tobe later, or send after him. The days of sitting here waiting had not improved Son's disposition much; he still prowled suspiciously, growled when spoken to and walked around like a crown prince waiting for the coronation.

It'll be worth half my wages to dump him in the old man's lap and then kiss him goodbye with the toe of my boot, Dundee thought.

He could see two riders slowly stringing the cattle along the creek. He could pick out Warren McCown by the way he sat his horse. The other man was a stranger, evidently a cowboy Warren had picked up to help him drive the herd. Dundee splashed the horse across the creek and rode up to Warren, his hand raised in the peace sign.

The bearded Warren nodded, eyes friendly. "Howdy,

Dundee. If you want to check the brands, just help yourself.''

"I don't reckon that'll be necessary."

"Do it anyway. Then you can tell old John Titus that I got none of his cattle here, and you can vouch for me."

Dundee rough-counted about a hundred mother cows. They carried two brands he had never seen before.

Warren said, "I can show you the bills of sale."

"You don't have to."

"I will anyway." Warren pulled them out of his pocket and extended them at arm's length. "Just in case anybody asks you."

Dundee nodded. Then he shoved his hand forward. "Pleased to see you back, Warren."

Suspicion crept into Warren's eyes. "How come you to know I'd been gone?"

"I been at your place several days."

Warren tried not to show it, but Dundee could see the sudden worry. "How's Millie?" Dundee could tell there was more Warren wanted to ask, but he wouldn't do it, not in words.

"She's fine."

"I don't like to go off and leave her there, just her and Uncle Ollie."

"Nobody's bothered her, Warren. I'll vouch for that."

Dundee could feel the keen probing of Warren's eyes, until Warren at last appeared satisfied. Dundee said: "I found her needing help, so I stayed. Uncle Ollie got himself hurt." He remembered the story the girl and the old man had made up for Warren. "Fell off of a horse. Was too shook up to do much for himself. He's better now, though."

Warren's eyes narrowed. "More than likely fell out of a rocking chair, if the truth was known. He's like my old daddy used to be, a gypsy. He'd starve to death if he didn't have somebody to lean on." Warren paused, embarrassed. "Sorry, Dundee. I know you got no interest in our family problems. I think the world of Uncle Ollie, but I know where his weakness is. I been fighting it all my life, in him, in my old daddy . . . even in myself."

Dundee shrugged. "Anyway, I can afford to leave now that you're home."

Warren stared at him a minute, silent. "Thanks for helping Millie. You didn't have to do it."

"I couldn't of left."

Warren frowned. "And I expect I know why. I could see it, the way you looked at her, the way she looked back at you. You're not for her, Dundee. She needs a man, and she'll get herself one. But you're not the kind, and I think you know it."

"You figure I got some gypsy in me, too?"

"You're not lazy, the way Uncle Ollie is. But you got a restlessness about you. You'll never stay put. Millie needs a man who'll make a home for her and stay there."

"I been wondering if maybe I could change."

"A colt may change color, but a grown horse never does."

They loose-herded the cattle along the creek awhile until the animals settled down and began to graze. Finally satisfied they would stay, Warren signaled the cowboy and pointed toward the house. The rider crossed the creek and waited on the other side. Warren introduced Dundee to him. "We'll treat him to a woman-cooked meal before he heads for home. He's been a lot of help."

The cowboy had nothing much to say. Dundee measured him with his eyes and decided the cowboy would probably take his wages and head for the nearest town to blow them in. That, in all likelihood, would be Runaway. He would ride out of there broke, sadder, but probably not wiser. Dundee knew. *He* had done the same thing more times than he cared to remember.

On the way in, Dundee recounted old Roan's bringing Son Titus.

Warren jerked his head around in surprise. "Son Titus, in *my* house?"

"I hope you don't mind."

Warren frowned deeply. "He's there, so I guess it don't make any difference. But old John Titus looks on all of us as cowthieves. I sure never expected to see any of his kin staying in my house."

"I'm figuring on getting him out pretty quick." Dundee paused. "I better warn you: he ain't the most likable sort you ever met. Chances are he'll insult you before you get out of the saddle."

"Then I'll probably hit him."

"Probably. I want you to know there won't be no hard feelings on my part."

"Wouldn't change things none if there was."

Dundee guessed that was why he had come to like Warren McCown. Warren had a way of saying what he thought, whether it crawled under your hide or not. Maybe sometime Dundee could bring John Titus around to meet him. The old ranchman appreciated a man who could stand flat-footed and tell him to go to hell.

Millie McCown threw her arms around her brother, paying no attention to two weeks' ragged growth of beard. Warren tolerated her tears for a smiling moment, then reminded her how hungry he and the cowboy were. She begged him to tell her about his trip.

"Nothing to tell," he said. "We come a long ways. No excitement. Now we're mighty lank and looking for something to eat."

Son Titus had been poking around somewhere back of the house. He came up now as if the place belonged to him. He stopped at the corner and stared distrustfully at Warren McCown and the cowboy.

Warren's eyes narrowed a little. "Hello, Son Titus."

Son appeared puzzled. "I don't know you. How come you know me?"

"It don't matter. I know you."

Neither made a move to shake hands. Dundee said, "Son, this is Warren McCown."

Son said: "I figured that. He's got a little the same looks as the girl, only not a bit pretty. Did you get a good look at the brands on them cattle?"

Warren answered for Dundee, his voice tight. "He did. And I also showed him the bills of sale. You want to see them too, Son? If you do, all you got to do is come and take them away from me."

Dundee guessed he ought to stop this before it went any

farther, but he didn't make a move. It would be pleasureful to see Son Titus take a stomping.

Millie was the one who headed it off. "Warren, there's hot coffee on the stove. I expect it'd taste pretty good while you wait for me to cook some dinner."

Warren gave Son Titus a hard glance. "All right, Millie. I expect it would." He walked on into the cabin, the cowboy following. Dundee strode angrily toward Son Titus.

"Son, I wisht I knew what it is that ails you. That's a hell of a way to talk to a man after you've enjoyed the hospitality of his house."

"I ain't enjoyed it very much. You're keeping me prisoner."

"You're not a prisoner. You were wondering about them cattle. Why don't you saddle up and go look at them for yourself? You're free to ride."

"You're a slick one, ain't you? You know I ain't fixing to ride very far from here without a gun, and I know you got mine hid someplace."

"You'll get it back when I turn you over to your old daddy."

"I want it now."

"Fiddle with me very much and I'll give you something you *don't* want."

"You'll have to have a heap of help." Son turned on his heel and stalked toward the saddleshed. After several paces he stopped and looked back over his shoulder. "I *will* go see them cattle. Don't hold your breath waiting for me to come back. I'll be awhile."

"Take all the time you want to." The longer he was gone, Dundee figured, the quieter it would be around here.

Son didn't come in for dinner. Warren's cowboy collected his pay, burped happily and left in the general direction of Runaway, as Dundee had expected. A good deal later Son Titus came in. Dundee should have been warned by the triumph in his eyes. But Dundee was enjoying a minor triumph of his own. "You see them cattle all right?"

"I seen them."

"Satisfied they ain't from the T Bar?"

"I reckon."

"Next time maybe you won't be so hell-bent to accuse everybody."

"Maybe not."

Dundee stared in puzzlement as Son walked on by him toward the kitchen. It had been too easy. Up to now Dundee hadn't really won a single argument with Son, except that one in Titusville, and even there it had been a victory of muscle rather than will. In the days they had been here at the McCown place, Son had contested Dundee on almost everything he talked about except the weather. The only thing that had held Son here had been the knowledge that Dundee could clean his plow. As it was, Son stayed around on the edge of things, watching suspiciously from afar, coming in to eat or visit a little with the recuperating Tobe Crane, then drifting off by himself to simmer like a pot of beans at the back of the stove. He even kept his blankets out at the saddleshed and slept apart from the others.

Mostly Dundee had watched his eyes.

The whole time we been here, he's been dreaming up ways to even the score with me, Dundee thought. *Maybe now he thinks he's got something that'll work. He'll bear watching.*

And Dundee watched him, till at dusk Son strayed off toward the corrals as he always did, to sleep alone. To reassure himself, Dundee dug down through the wood in the big box behind the stove, till he found the six-shooters where he had put them. That eased his mind somewhat, for he had begun to suspect that Son might have found his gun.

Next morning Son didn't come in for breakfast. Dundee walked out to the corrals to fetch him and came hurrying back, breath short from running. "Anybody hear a horse leave last night?"

Warren McCown shook his head. "Son Titus run out on you, Dundee?"

"He's gone ... horse, saddle and all."

McCown smiled thinly. "Can't say it grieves me much."

"It grieves the hell out of *me*. I can't figure him going off without a gun. . . ." A sudden thought struck him like he had been kicked by a yearling. ''Warren, that cowboy with you yesterday . . . he was wearing a gun. . . .''

McCown nodded. ''A .45, I think it was.''

''Son didn't come in till an hour or so after your cowboy left here. I bet he waited out yonder someplace, stopped that feller and bought the gun off of him.'' Dundee choked down some words he thought Millie was too young to hear.

''Whichaway do you reckon he went?''

''I'll hunt for his tracks, but I think I already know.''

He didn't bother trying to follow the trail. The destination was plain enough: Runaway. Dundee put the bay horse into a steady trot, his mind running wild with all manner of notions about the trouble Son Titus could have gotten himself into by now. He saw him being shot, knifed, stomped, clubbed and dragged at the end of a rope. It wouldn't displease Dundee to see any of these things happen to the fool kid, except that most of them were inclined to be so damned permanent.

He stopped at the crest of the hill and looked down over the motley stretch of the town, wondering which picket shack or rock saloon he would find Son Titus in . . . if any of them. By now the button might be lying dead on that riverbank someplace, cast out there like the empty bottles and rusting cans and bleaching cartridge boxes which littered the place, giving mute testimony to many a day and night of revelry and devilment in times past. Though he didn't want to, Dundee gazed a moment at the mercantile across from the Llano River Saloon, coldness touching him as he remembered Bunch Karnes slumping in a lifeless heap on the dirt street in front of it.

He reined up at the wagonyard, stood in his stirrups and peered over the picket fence, studying the horses penned there. He picked out the sorrel that Son Titus had ridden. Son was still here, then. At least, he hadn't left here horseback.

The liveryman was forking hay into a bunk made of cedar pickets. He stood the fork against a fence and came walking, taking his time. ''Howdy.'' From the man's eyes

Dundee knew he was recognized. "Something I can do for you, friend?"

Dundee pointed with his chin. "That sorrel yonder . . . what do you know about him?"

"Just that he's a horse." The man shrugged. "He's got a T Bar brand on him. Boy come in here last night, said he was old John Titus' son. I figured if he was telling the truth, fine. If he wasn't, stolen horses ain't no lookout of mine. Either way, *my* nose don't get skinned."

"You seen that boy this morning?"

"Nope."

"You know where he went?"

"I keep horses, that's all."

Dundee frowned. "Did you hear any shooting last night?"

"There's shooting most *every* night. Most times it's just in fun. Long's it don't hurt me none, I don't pay it any mind."

Dryly Dundee said, "Thanks, friend, you been real helpful." He headed the bay down the crooked street in a walk, gazing suspiciously at every shack as he passed it. He didn't know just what he was looking for. Whatever it was, he didn't find it. When he reached the far end of town he had seen nothing that would help him locate Son Titus. He started back.

His gaze fell upon Katy Long's Llano River Saloon and, inevitably, upon the place in the dirt where Bunch Karnes had fallen. A dun horse had stood hitched there quite a while, evidently, and he had left the sign of time's slow passage on the spot where Karnes' blood had soaked into the earth.

They don't honor death here much more than they honor life, Dundee thought.

He dismounted at the saloon and looked around a moment, warily gauging the prospect of a reception. There was none that he could see. But a tingling along his spine told him he wasn't being overlooked. He stretched to get the saddle-stiffness out of his muscles, then stepped into the saloon.

Katy Long sat at a table riffling a deck of cards. She gazed up at Dundee with the faintest suggestion of a smile. He would swear she was laughing at him. "What kept you?" she asked. "Son Titus got to town before midnight."

"I sleep late." He looked beyond her to the hallway. "I don't reckon he'd be in here someplace?"

She shook her head. "How'd he get out of his cage?"

"I forgot the lock. If he's not in here, where you reckon he's at?"

She continued to smile. "You were his age once. Where would you have gone?" When he didn't answer, she added, "You'll find them down the street, *way* down the street."

"How'll I know them?"

"You're old enough. You'll know them."

Dundee stared at this woman who seemed to enjoy sticking needles in him. "Last time I implied some things about *you,* you got awful mad," he said.

"I got mad because they weren't true. But you're not mad; you're smiling."

Dundee realized that he was, and he tried to put a stop to it. "You've made a big point about how all you sell is whisky. Will you sell me a drink?"

She said: "I sure hadn't figured on *giving* you one. Cricket, fetch Dundee some of our best. I figure he can afford it."

Dundee said: "I'll drink whatever old Roan Hardesty does. He ought to know his liquor."

She shook her head. "Don't take him for a model. He'll drink anything but coal oil. Sit down, Dundee."

"I figured one drink, then I'd go hunt for Son Titus."

"He's all right. If anything had happened to him, I'd have heard. You can take time to sit down and enjoy the whisky."

Dundee looked at the layout of the windows and moved to the other side of the table where the bar and a solid wall would be to his back.

Katy Long's smile faded. "You act like you've been in towns like this before."

"Not many, I'm glad to say. Mostly I've just cowboyed.

It don't pay too good, but a man's back is safe." He seated himself, took the drink the bartender had put on the table in front of him and downed it. He frowned darkly. "If this is your good whisky, I'm glad I didn't ask for nothing cheap."

"We don't get a very choosy clientele here."

"Maybe you would, if you'd handle a better line of goods."

"You want to try it? I'd sell you the place cheap."

"It wouldn't be a good long-range investment, not here in Runaway."

"You don't think Runaway has a bright future?"

"And not very *long*, either. I figure old John Titus has got some plans for Runaway, and they ain't likely to be good for the whisky business. If somebody comes along and wants to buy this place, you sell it to him."

Her eyebrows went up a little. "How come you interested in my welfare, Dundee?"

He shrugged. "I don't put no burrs under my blanket, either way. But seeing how you patched up that Crane boy and Son Titus, I don't see no harm in trying to help you out of the gully before the flood comes down."

"You know how hard it is to kill a snake. Runaway won't die easy."

"John Titus has got it wrote down at the top of his list."

She was silent a time. "Well, I came by the place awfully cheap. I don't have a lot to lose." Her eyes narrowed. "Besides, John Titus may not be as tough as you think he is."

"Don't bet on it. If you get yourself an offer, sell." He pushed his chair back. "Enjoyed the hospitality, Miss Long." He realized it was the first time he had called her that—or anything, really—in a respectful manner. "I'd best go find the cub and fetch him home."

"You be careful, Dundee. There's people here who would be tickled to death to pitch in and help pay for your funeral."

"I'll try to save them their money."

He stopped outside the door and took a long look up the street, then down. Again, he wasn't quite sure what he was looking for, but he figured he'd know when he saw it. The death of Bunch Karnes across the street was still on his mind, and he knew it hadn't been forgotten by the people around here, either. He swung into the saddle and started back down the street. He tried not to give the appearance of looking for trouble, but his eyes kept moving. He didn't intend to miss anything.

Down at the far end of town he'd seen a couple of long, narrow frame buildings that had not known the luxury of paint, though he'd seen a woman staring out a window who *had*. He could remember when such a place would have held fascination for him, and he reasoned it might be so for Son Titus. He swung down at the first house, tied the horse and walked in. The odor of cheap perfume and whisky and greasy cooking struck him across the face like a wet saddleblanket. A woman stood at an ironing board, pressing a dress with a heated flatiron. She was perhaps thirty or so, dressed in nothing but a shift, sweat trickling down her surprised face, her blondish hair hanging in untended strings. Plainly, this wasn't during business hours.

"Mister," she said irritably, "don't you know what time it is? It's the middle of the day."

"I'm looking for a man."

"Most people come in here, they ain't looking for no *man*. There's none here."

Dundee looked past her at a long hallway that had small rooms leading off to one side. "I think I'll go and see for myself."

Face clouding, the woman raised her hand. "Not unless you want a faceful of hot iron, you don't."

She had *somebody* back there she didn't want seen, he figured. "You put that iron down or I'm liable to lay it against your broad rump and brand you like a white-faced heifer!"

She placed the iron back on the board. He started down the hall, opening doors, the woman following along cursing him. There were four doors, altogether. Inside the last room he found a man, but not Son Titus. Old Roan Hardesty was caught with his dignity down. He bawled,

"Dammit, Dundee, didn't nobody ever teach you how to knock on a door?"

Dundee said, "Didn't go to bother you."

The woman was still cursing when he walked back to the front room. Dundee laid a few pieces of silver on the ironing board. "Buy yourself a bottle."

He was glad to get into fresh air again, but he knew the next house wouldn't be any better than this one. He stopped at the front door a moment, wishing he had another drink to fortify himself. These places were hell in the daylight.

Son Titus sat in the small parlor in a settee, his bare feet propped up on a soft chair, a bottle in his right hand, his left arm hugging a small blonde girl tightly against him. Son grinned with triumph. "Come in this house, Dundee. You're later than I figured you'd be. Old age must be slowing you down."

"I'm not too old, button."

"Well, then, I bet Lutie here can find you a friend."

"All I came for was *you,* and I ain't calling you friend."

"You sound mad, Dundee. You'd of done the same in my place."

"Get up and put your boots on, Son Titus. I'm taking you back."

Son Titus squeezed the girl. "I ain't going back. I like it fine right here with Lutie." The girl smiled at Son and pouted at Dundee. He could tell she had looked into that bottle a good many times.

Dundee pointed down the hall. He noticed this house was built just like the other one. "Girl, you go back yonder and find yourself something to do. I got business with Son."

Son Titus said: "I got no business with you, Dundee. I like it fine, right where I'm at."

Dundee spoke severely to the blonde, "I told you once already, get yourself out of here!"

Eyes wide, the girl got up, tightened her wrapper and weaved down the hall, anxiously looking backward, bumping her shoulder.

Son Titus brought his bare feet to the hooked rug. "Dundee, I'm getting awful tired of you."

"I ain't having much fun with you, either. Put your boots on."

Glaring, Son Titus set the nearly-empty bottle on a small table. His fists knotted. "What if I don't?"

"Then you'll go barefooted."

"I mean, what if I tell you I ain't going atall?"

Dundee took a long breath and let it out slowly in exasperation. "Son, you're too drunk to put up a good fight. But I will fight you if I have to. I'll whip you like I whipped you that night in Titusville, and I'll enjoy myself every minute of it."

Son pushed to his feet. "You want to start now?"

The blonde girl hurried back down the hall, bringing with her a large, raw-boned woman with red hair who looked like a sister of the woman in the other house. The woman shouted: "No you don't! I ain't putting up with no fighting in my house. It cost me a wagonload of money for the furniture in here, and I won't allow no brawling drunks to go busting it up."

Must have been an awful little wagon, Dundee thought, looking at the old settee, the old painted table, the kerosene lamps.

Dundee nodded. "All right, Son, if you got to have it, we'll go outside and settle things."

Son's boots lay where he had kicked them off, in a corner. To put them on without sitting down, he had to stand on first one leg, then the other. Watching him, Dundee decided the button wasn't really very drunk, for he managed the job handily.

Dundee had known the time when he enjoyed a fistfight; it limbered him up, roused his blood into good circulation, quickened his heart like a big shot of whisky. Now he felt no relish for it. Not even getting to whip Son Titus seemed worth the effort. But if the job was to be done, he'd best be getting on with it, so he could put this infernal town behind him. He walked out the door and into the street. He glanced at his horse and moved well away from the bay. A horse could be a fool over something like a fistfight. Dundee chose a place and stood waiting for Son Titus to come out.

Son took his time. When he moved through the door, his step was steady, his eyes alert. Dundee wondered if he'd been drinking anything out of that bottle or if he'd just pretended and had been trying only to get the girl drunk.

Maybe he's shrewder than I figured him out to be.

Son's gaze touched Dundee, then darted away. He was reaching for his pistol as he shouted, "Look out, Dundee!"

Instinctively Dundee jumped aside, not sure whether Son Titus was about to shoot him or was going for someone else. A bullet smashed into the frame house even as he heard the crash of a rifle behind him. Dundee whirled, hand darting down and coming up with his six-shooter. Son Titus fired at someone across the street before Dundee got turned. Dundee caught a glimpse of a man at the corner of a picket-and-sod shack, feverishly levering another cartridge into the breech of his smoking rifle. Dundee fired once, knowing he was moving too fast and the distance was too much. He saw the slug kick dust from the shack's wall. Son Titus fired again, chipping wood from a picket just over the man's head. The bushwhacker brought the rifle up again, but he was flustered now with two men shooting at him. Dundee ran, zigzagging. The rifle flashed, but the bullet missed. The man turned and fled, limping badly.

Son Titus hollered, "Let's get him, Dundee!"

Dundee shouted back: "You stay right where you're at! I ain't packing you home dead!"

Dundee raced toward the shack. He could see the man ahead of him, running stiff-legged toward a horse, a little too far for Dundee to hit him. The man swung into the saddle and spurred hard, the rifle still in his hand. Dundee took one more shot at him, knowing he was throwing lead away but figuring he would feel better about it if he at least made the try.

He stopped then to catch his breath, letting the smoking pistol hang at arm's length. He cursed a little because he was angrier than he was scared. He knew who had shot at him: Jason Karnes, brother of Bunch Karnes; Jason Karnes, who had caught Dundee's bullet in his leg in a cowthief camp.

Looks like I'll be forced to put another bullet in him before this is over with, Dundee told himself regretfully. *I'll have to place that next one a mite higher up*.

Son Titus said proudly, "Well, we run him off, didn't we, Dundee?"

Dundee nodded, sober. "I reckon we did. Thanks, Son. If you hadn't hollered, he'd of probably taken me with that first shot."

Son said, "Then I reckon you owe me something."

"I reckon. What?"

"Go off and leave me alone. I ain't finished all my business with Lutie, and you're sure putting a crimp in things."

Dundee frowned. "Son, I'd do anything I rightly could to pay you back. But if I was to leave you here, I wouldn't be doing you no favor. No sir, you're coming on with me the way we started."

Son's voice flattened. "You mean after what I done for you . . ."

"After what you done for me, you're still going back to your old daddy. Now get your horse."

"Like hell I will!"

He stood there within easy reach, and Dundee didn't feel like a prolonged argument. He put his pistol back into the holster, balled his right hand into a fist and brought it up with all his strength behind it. It caught Son flatfooted, but it didn't leave him that way. He lay on his back in the street, shaking his head and blinking.

Son rubbed his jaw, flinching from the unexpected pain. "I swear, Dundee, you sure hit a man hard."

"It helps shorten an argument."

Son's eyes were glazed a little. "If I hadn't saved your life, you'd of been mad at me. I *did* save it, and you won't do me a favor."

"I *am* doing you a favor. I'm getting you out of Runaway while your health is good."

IX

As they topped the hill, Son Titus looked back over his shoulder at Runaway below. "I wasn't finished down there."

"Yes, you was," Dundee said.

That was the last Son Titus spoke for many miles. He rode along with his head down, sleeping on horseback. It suited Dundee all right, for so long as Son was asleep he wasn't belly-aching.

I ought to charge old John Titus double for this job, he thought. *Hunting cowthieves is what I hired for. I didn't come here to wetnurse a chuckleheaded button.*

But now and again he would glance at the relaxed face of Son Titus and feel something vaguely akin to liking. Son could have stood there and let Karnes shoot him, but he hadn't. He had pitched in. Maybe it wasn't because he felt any desire to help Dundee; maybe he just wanted the excitement. No matter; if it hadn't been for Son Titus, Dundee knew he'd probably be the cause of somebody having to do a job of digging in the rocky ground that was Runaway's Boothill.

Son Titus stirred finally. He blinked, shut his eyes a while, blinked some more and came awake. His face twisted as he worked up spittle and tried to clear his mouth of a bad taste. "How far we come?"

"A ways. You ought to swear off of whisky."

"Truth is, *she* done most of the drinking. I didn't really drink much. Just a few little snorts."

Dundee had sort of guessed that.

Son said: "I figured a girl like her would hear lots of things. Figured if she got to drinking it'd loosen her tongue up, and then maybe I'd find out something."

"Did it work thataway?"

"Some. Mostly it made her affectionate. Of course, there wasn't nothing wrong with *that*, neither."

"What did you find out, when she wasn't being affectionate?"

"Found out a little about you, Dundee. Found out they're scared of you in Runaway."

"Did that convince you I ain't no cowthief?"

"Why else you reckon I'd've bothered to holler at you when that feller was fixing to let air through your brisket?"

"I sort of wondered."

"Well, it wasn't on account of your good looks and disposition."

At length they came to a creek, its clear water gurgling over the big polished stones that lay in its shallow bed. Son Titus licked his lips. "Last night I wouldn't of give you a nickel for all the water in Kingdom Come. Now it's worth ten dollars a gallon. I'm going to step down and drink up about a hundred dollars worth."

Son dropped on his belly and stretched out over the creek's bank, cupping the palm of his right hand to bring water up so he didn't have to dip his face under. He drank long and thirstily, pausing only to catch his breath.

"Ain't you afraid that stuff'll rust your gut?" Dundee asked.

"Not with the coating I put on it last night."

Dundee watered the horses. Son Titus finally seemed satisfied. He pushed to his feet, wiping his sleeve across his mouth. "Nectar of the gods. You ought to try it, Dundee."

Dundee hadn't noticed being thirsty, but he guessed it was the power of suggestion, watching Son Titus, "It's a ways yet to the next water. I reckon maybe I will."

He stretched out on the bank, a little above where Titus had lain. He was drinking when he heard Son's saddle creak and felt the reins jerked from his left hand. He rolled over and jumped to one knee. Son Titus was riding his own horse and leading Dundee's up the creekbank. Out of reach, Son paused to look back. "Go on and drink your fill, Dundee. You got lots of time."

"You bring my horse back here, Son Titus!"

"I hope you're a good walker, Dundee. It's a far piece back to Runaway, or out to McCown's, whichever way you decide to go. Me, *I* could tell you where to go."

"Son Titus. . . ."

"Like I said, Dundee, I ain't finished all my business in Runaway yet. That's where you'll find your horse." He swung his sorrel around and led the bay. "Adios, Dundee. Enjoy yourself."

"You crazy button, I'll. . . ." Dundee broke off as he watched Son ride away laughing, into the lengthening shadows. He hurled his hat to the ground. He wanted to stomp it, but that wouldn't have been enough. One of these days he'd stomp Son Titus instead. Times, he wished he'd never strayed through Titusville, had never seen old John Titus or Son. He ought to turn his back on the whole damned mess and let them steal the T Bar blind.

But he knew he was in it too far to pull out now. He'd follow on through. But one of these days, when it was over. . . .

He clenched his fists and recited Son Titus' ancestry for several generations back.

Dundee was a cowboy, and cowboys seldom walked. It was contrary to their religion. A cowboy would descend into many types of sin before he would risk blisters on his feet. Dundee considered the distance. It might be a little shorter to the McCown place than to Runaway, but not enough to offset the time it would take to get a horse at McCown's and ride all the way back. Another thing, the trail back to Runaway was easier followed in the dark.

Muttering, he climbed the creekbank. He slipped, caught himself, hurled a rock as far as he could throw it and started the long walk.

The night was far gone when he finally got to Runaway. Legs aching, feet blistered and sore, his anger simmering like bitter roots being boiled for backwoods medicine, he dragged himself up to the front gate of the wagonyard. Down the street he could see most of the buildings standing dark. A lantern still flickered in front of the Llano

River Saloon, one at another bar farther along. Way down at the end of the street he saw a dim red glow.

The small barn was dark. Well, by George, if *he* was awake, everybody else had just as well be. "Hey!" he shouted. "Where's the man that runs this place?"

He heard a grumbling from a blanket spread on hay in the corner. He struck a match and held it down close. The drunken face he saw there, the eyes blinking in confusion, did not belong to the man he was looking for. "Hey! Stableman, wake up!"

From another corner he heard the squeak of steel cotsprings as a man turned over on his blankets. "You damned drunks . . . you won't let a sober man get no sleep. Go find your own horse and leave me be."

In the reflected moonlight Dundee made out a lantern. He lighted it and turned up the wick. "I ain't drunk."

The yardman swung his bare feet off to the ground. He was wearing long underwear, only half buttoned. He yawned, then peered irritably at Dundee. "Oh, it's you. You'll find your horse in the corral and your saddle on the fence. That button left them here."

"How long ago?"

"I don't know. I been asleep."

"Is his horse here too?"

"He kept his. Just left yours."

"Whichaway did he go this time?"

"Like I told you before, I don't notice nothing that ain't my business. That way my health stays good. Now, take your horse and get out of here so I can go back to bed."

Dundee saddled, swung up and started to ride down the street. The yardman met him, still barefoot and in the longhandles. "Wait, cowboy, you owe me a hay bill."

"How much?"

"Two bits. I ought to charge you extra for waking me up."

Dundee dug for it. A thought struck him. "You heard any shooting in town since that boy came in?"

The stableman held the coin into the moonlight and fingered it suspiciously. "Since you ask me, I heard a couple shots down the street."

"Do you know what happened?"

"Yep. I turned over and went back to sleep."

Dundee rode down the dark street, glad to be off of his sore feet and glad most of the town was asleep. He hoped Jason Karnes was, too. To be on the safe side, he reached down and drew the carbine from its scabbard.

Keeping out of the lantern's glow, he peered inside the Llano River Saloon. He saw the bulky figure of Roan Hardesty hunched over a table studying a hand of cards. Opposite him, Katy Long sat waiting for him to make his play. Best Dundee could tell, most of the chips were on her side.

Dundee rode to the house where he had found Son Titus the last time. He didn't see Son's horse tied anywhere. The house was dark now, except for the glow of a lantern in one of the rooms in the far back. Dundee walked partway back for a look-see, but a curtain was drawn across the window. He returned to the front, pushed the door open and walked in.

"Son Titus! You in here?" No reply. "Son Titus, I come to get you!"

He heard movement down the hall. He brought the carbine up, just in case. A door opened and lamplight came floating toward him, a long shadow preceding a woman. She stopped, the lamp in her hand, her eyes blinking in sleepiness. "What's going on in here? Don't you know what time it is? Decent folks are all asleep."

It was the same red-haired, raw-boned woman he had crossed before. Her stringy hair and the pouches under her eyes didn't help her looks any. Dundee said: "Son Titus came back in here tonight. I want him."

The woman scowled. "He ain't here."

Dundee saw no reason to accept her word. "Where's that girl he was with, the one called Lutie?"

"Lutie's asleep. You ain't going to bother her."

"I asked where she's at." Dundee took two long steps toward the woman. She began to retreat. "Now, mister. . . ."

"I'll find her if I have to tear this place apart. Her and him both. Now, where's she at?"

Grumbling, the woman turned down the hallway, still

carrying the lamp. "She's back thisaway. But you ain't going to find out much talking to her."

She opened a door and pointed. The girl lay across a brass bed, her loose gown pulled halfway up her legs, the blanket thrown off.

"Lutie," Dundee demanded, "Where's Son Titus?"

The girl stirred but never opened her eyes. Dundee noticed a bottle lying by the bed. It was empty.

The woman said: "That friend of yours, he brought that bottle with him. Must of let her drink most of it by herself. Time he left here, she was so drunk you'd of thought he'd hit her with a sledge. She won't be worth nothing for two days. It's a sin the way that girl likes whisky. It'll be the ruin of her one of these times."

Dundee grasped the girl's shoulder and shook her. "Lutie, I want to find Son Titus."

The girl moaned, but that was all.

The woman said: "Like I told you, you ain't going to get nothing out of her. She's too drunk."

Dundee stepped back, hand tight on the carbine. Where would he go from here?

"How long's Son been gone?"

"Must've been midnight . . . one o'clock. After he left, I came to see about Lutie. This is the way I found her." She glared. "When you find that Titus, you tell him I don't want him back in here again, ever. He's a bad influence on my girls."

Dundee turned to go. "One more thing. Feller told me he heard some shooting tonight. Was that before Son left, or after?"

The red-haired woman rubbed a hand across her face, trying to remember. "There's always some drunk shooting a pistol around here. I expect it was Titus done it. He left here looking awful satisfied with himself."

Dundee glanced once more at Lutie. *I'll bet.*

Frustrated, uncertain, Dundee walked outside. At the house next door, a woman stepped to the little porch and blew out a red lantern, then retreated inside. That was the house Dundee had searched yesterday, looking for Son Titus. He considered looking again, but he figured Son wouldn't have left Lutie's place to go to another just like it. Dundee looked up the street. The only light he could see now was the single lantern in front of Katy Long's saloon. The rest of the town was in its blankets.

Dundee swung onto the bay and rode back up there. He tied the horse in the darkness and walked around to the rear of the place. He found a rear door and tried it. It was unlocked. He entered the dark hall and carefully made his way along it, guided by the moonlight through the windows. At the door leading into the main room of the saloon, he stopped to look for a moment before stepping into the lamplight. He saw only two people: Katy Long and old Blue Roan. Roan was gulping a shot of whisky and watching Katy rake in another pile of chips.

Dundee said, "You ought to know better than to gamble with a good-looking woman."

Roan turned quickly, surprised. His hand dropped toward his pistol, then stopped as his blinking eyes recognized Dundee. Katy Long was startled, but she never moved.

Roan recovered his composure. "How come, Dundee? I'd rather play cards with a good-looking woman than with any of the ugly men I've gambled with."

"Hard to keep your mind on the cards."

Katy Long said evenly: "I believe that's the first compliment you've paid me, Dundee. You must want something."

"I want Son Titus. Where's he at?"

She smiled thinly. "You'd make a mighty poor jailer, Dundee. Can't even keep one tight-britches kid under control."

'He was in here, wasn't he?''

She nodded. "Bought another bottle, early in the evening. Said you'd probably come in sometime during the night. Enjoy your walk, Dundee?"

He ignored the barb. "My feet are sore and my patience is run out. I want to know if you saw Son Titus anymore after he bought that bottle?"

"Nope. You'll probably find him where you found him yesterday."

"I already looked. He left."

"Then there's not much telling. Maybe he went home."

"Shots were fired somewhere on the street a while ago. What were they?"

Katy glanced at old Roan, and both of them shrugged. Roan said: "Some drunk, most likely. I didn't hear any more commotion, so I didn't go look." He added ruefully, "I was winning at the time."

Dundee glanced at the pile of chips in front of the woman. "That must've been a *long* while ago."

Katy said seriously: "Dundee, he probably went home. You look like you need sleep. I can fix you up with a cot back yonder. You can go find him in the morning."

"I'll sleep after I've found him. I think I'll tie him to a wagonwheel with wet rawhide and then sleep while the hide dries."

Roan said: "I still got orders out, Dundee. Nobody hurts him."

"Does everybody obey your orders?"

"Not always."

"That's why I got to find him before some of your boys do. If they haven't already."

Dundee turned to go. His tired legs betrayed him, and he almost fell. Roan Hardesty's big mouth turned downward sourly. "He just thinks he's going someplace. You better bed him down, Katy. Next time I'll get them chips on *my* side of the table again."

She smiled. "Glad to give you the chance. Bring lots of money."

"I always do. But I seldom leave here with any." He looked at Dundee. "Wherever that boy's at, he'll keep till daylight. You rest yourself. Where's your horse?"

"Out back."

"I'll drop him off at the wagonyard. Good night, Katy."

"Good night, Roan."

Dundee slumped in a chair and watched Katy Long rake the poker chips into a small leather bag. "You always beat him like that?"

"I let him win now and again, so he doesn't lose hope."

"Crafty, ain't you?"

"I've been taking care of myself in a man's world for a good many years now. I think I know how." She counted and stacked more chips, glancing up occasionally at Dundee. She had poker player's eyes; he couldn't tell what she was thinking. Finally she said: "You're really worried about that thick-headed kid, aren't you?"

"I'm mad enough to chew up nails and spit them in his face."

"But worried, just the same?"

He nodded.

She said: "You know, Dundee, the first time I saw you I figured you were just another tough drifter with a cartridge case where your heart ought to be. But I believe I misjudged you. Times, you're damn near human."

She arose, walked to the front and blew out the lantern that hung on the porch. She shut the door and came back, lighting a lamp that sat on the end of the bar. "Blow out that overhead lamp for me. Then come on back and I'll show you a bed."

He followed her out of the dark saloon and into the hall. She opened the door to the room where she had treated Jason Karnes' wound so many weeks ago. He said: "I'll sleep awhile, then slip out. I'll try not to make any fuss when I go."

She stood in the doorway, holding the lamp. Dundee stared at her a moment, a strong urge building in him. He reached up and took her chin and kissed her. She backed off a step, surprised.

"What was that for?"

"I just wanted to do it."

Her eyes studied him unflinchingly. "Comparing me to that country girl?"

"That's not it. . . ."

"Well, do I measure up?"

He shook his head, not knowing what to say. "It's like I told you out yonder that day . . . I haven't touched her. I. . . ."

"You've wanted to."

"Sure I've wanted to. I just ain't done it."

"So you come to me, figuring anything you do to me is all right."

Angering, he said: "I didn't mean to get your hackles

up. I don't have to sleep here if you don't want me to. I'll just go on like I'd figured to in the first place.''

She stared at him awhile longer, and he thought he saw the laughter come back into her eyes. She blew out the lamp and set it on a table. She said: ''Empty talk, Dundee. You're not a man to start something and not finish it. You'll stay right here.''

X

He was up at daylight, dressing quietly to try to keep from awakening Katy Long. But the tinkle of a spur rowel brought her eyes open. She reached out and caught his hand. Her sleepy eyes smiled. ''No goodbyes?''

''Hadn't figured on it. I got to find Son Titus.''

''You'll be back.''

''Better not count on it.''

She repeated confidently, ''You'll be back.''

He walked to the livery barn, where the yardman wanted to charge him another hay bill for the bay horse.

''I paid you once. He ain't been back here long enough to eat any more hay.''

''I put it out, and it gets eaten up. I don't know which ones eat it and which ones don't. So they all pay or they don't leave this corral.''

''You're a thief.''

''Who here ain't? Two bits, friend.''

Dundee paid him. The carbine across his lap, he rode down the street for another look by daylight. He saw nothing of Son Titus' sorrel. He rode around back and followed the alleyway, thinking he might find the horse tied somewhere there. That proved to be a waste of time. He scouted the riverbank, but still he found nothing.

Katy and Roan could have been right, he knew. Son could have gotten his fill of town and gone back to the McCown place. It might have been that he wanted to postpone facing up to Dundee for setting him afoot.

Those shots that had been fired during the night still nagged at him a little. True, the chances were it had been some cowboy sharing his celebration with the whole town. But there was always a chance. . . .

Dundee stopped and had breakfast in a saloon that doubled as a restaurant of sorts. He wondered if their whisky was as bad as their cooking and decided it probably was. He rode up the hill looking back over his shoulder, the carbine still across his lap as the sun started to climb. Then he lined out toward the McCown ranch, setting the bay into a steady trot.

It was late morning when he arrived. He rode straight for the saddleshed, looking for sign of Son's sorrel. The horse wasn't there. Well, he thought, maybe Son turned him loose to graze. After all, he'd put in an awful lot of miles. Dundee turned his bay out. He could borrow something from Warren if he had to ride again.

Millie McCown stood in the door, apron tied around her slender waist. Her eyes were wide as she watched him approach, but he could see relief in them. She stepped out to meet him, her hands forward to grasp him. "We were worried about you."

Her fingers were warm, but he pulled his hands away. He tried not to look at her. Remembering Katy Long, he found it hard to meet this girl's eyes. "I'm all right. Did Son Titus come back?"

"You mean you didn't find him?"

"I found him, then I lost him. He hasn't been here?"

She shook her head. "We haven't seen him."

The worry that had nagged him all the way out here descended on him like a dark and gloomy cloud. Of a sudden he was certain something had happened to Son Titus, something a lot worse than Dundee himself had planned to do to him.

In the cabin he found Tobe Crane sitting up on the edge of his cot, his sock feet on a small rug Millie had made.

Tobe's arm and shoulder were still tightly bound with clean white cloth. His face was pale, but it seemed to have more color in it than Dundee had seen before. "Dundee, you didn't find Son?"

Briefly Dundee told what had happened, though he left out those parts which might have brought a blush to Millie.

Tobe said: "Could be he was afraid to answer to you, Dundee. Could be he went straight back to his old daddy at the T Bar."

"Do you believe that, Tobe?"

Tobe shook his head. "Nope."

Dundee chewed the inside of his lip, his eyes narrowing. "I got a bad feeling about it. I can't put my finger on it, but I know. Harm's come to him."

Tobe pushed himself to his feet. "I'll help you find him." Tobe swayed, and for a moment it looked as if he would fall. Dundee rushed toward him, but Millie was closer. She grabbed Tobe and eased him back onto the cot, her face drained with sudden anxiety. "Tobe. . . ."

Dundee saw how Tobe clung to the girl's hand for a minute after he was on the cot. "You're not ready to go anywhere yet, Tobe."

Across the room, old Ollie McCown stiffly got up from a chair and hobbled a few steps toward Dundee. "I'll go with you. If somebody can help me get *on* a horse, I can ride him."

Dundee watched the old man till he was sure Ollie could do it. "Much obliged, Ollie. I'll be needing help. Where's Warren?"

Millie said: "He went out this morning to check on the new cattle and be sure they're not trying to drift south again. They do that, you know, till they get used to new range."

"You looking for him to come in to dinner?"

She nodded.

Dundee said: "Then we'll wait. Maybe three of us can locate Son."

They split at the creek, the three of them, each to scout a strip of the land that lay between there and Runaway.

Dundee himself took the middle one, where the trail ran, for he felt that was the most likely place. Possibly somebody had followed Son Titus out of town and waylaid him. Dundee crisscrossed back and forth, slowly working toward town. In the back of his mind those shots kept ringing, the ones he had heard about in Runaway.

If they'd killed Son, they perhaps had buried him by now. Old John Titus' boy might never be found. But then, there was Son's horse. Somewhere, somebody had to have that sorrel, and it would be a giveaway.

The sun was low when Dundee sat on the hill looking down upon Runaway. He had searched out its streets and alleys this morning, and the riverbank. But he hauled the carbine out of the scabbard and laid it across his lap, knowing he had to look again. He touched spurs to the dun horse he had borrowed from McCown.

Old Roan Hardesty sat on his big gray horse in the middle of the street and watched Dundee ride in. He glanced at the carbine, then shifted his gaze to Dundee's face. "Back again? You been here enough lately that you'd almost qualify to vote."

"I'm still looking for Son Titus. Do you know something you ought to tell me, Roan?"

The old outlaw appeared surprised. "You know as much as I do. I told you I give orders. . . ."

"And you told me not everybody obeys them orders."

"Son Titus ain't in Runaway, Dundee. If he was, I'd know it."

"But he *was* in Runaway, and he ain't showed up anyplace else. Don't that make you wonder, Roan?"

The old man looked genuinely regretful. "I wisht I knowed something to tell you." His gaze lifted. Dundee saw the blue spots seem to darken in the aging face as Roan stared past him. Dundee turned in the saddle. His blood went cold.

Two horsemen were coming down the hill, leading a third horse. It was a sorrel. And it had something tied across it.

Dundee turned his dun slowly around, his throat knotting. He didn't have to see any more. He knew.

Warren and Ollie McCown had found Son Titus, and
they were bringing him in.

Dundee sat slumped in the saddle, numb, as the two
riders came slowly down the street to meet him. At length
they reined in, their horses almost touching noses with his
dun. Dundee's gaze fastened on the slicker-wrapped bun-
dle tied across the trailing sorrel. He tried to speak, but his
throat was too full.

Warren McCown said quietly: "I found him out yonder,
a ways from town."

Old Roan Hardesty rode up closer, his face gray in
shock, the blue splotches standing out like tar spots.
"Dundee, I swear to you. . . ."

Dundee found his voice, and it was bitter. "Any swearing
you want to do, Roan, you better do it to old John Titus. I
expect you'll get the chance."

He turned his back on the big outlaw. "Warren, it's too
far to take him home to his old daddy. I'd like to bury
him on your place somewhere. It's sort of friendly ground."

Warren nodded soberly. "It's a long ways. We better get
started."

XI

Dundee had seen men die, but old John Titus was the first
he ever saw die and yet live. The ranchman scarcely
moved as Dundee told him, but the blood slowly drained
from his face, leaving it the color of ashes. The bright fire
of life seemed to die away and go to nothing more than
coals. The strong old hands knotted, the leaders standing
out like strands of rope. Dundee thought he heard a single
sobbing sound escape from John Titus' throat, but there
was no other, and he was never sure. For a long time the

old man sat there, blank eyes staring past Dundee into the infinity that only the mind can see.

Dundee wasn't sure the rancher was hearing him, but he went on and told the whole thing from beginning to end—most of it, anyway. At last he brought out the tally book and the map and laid them on the rolltop desk. Quietly he said: "I done what I set out to do, sir. I got it all here on paper, the just and the unjust alike."

The voice that spoke was not the same one which had welcomed Dundee at the door. It was a broken voice now, barely above a whisper. "Would you show me where you buried him, Dundee?"

"I'd want to, sir."

"There'll be more to do after that, Dundee. Will you stay with me?"

"I'd figured on it."

"You done real good." The old man's chin dropped a little. "Who was it you said owned the land you buried him on?"

"McCown, sir. The name's McCown."

"McCown." Titus seemed to test the word like he'd test a pot of beans.

"Maybe you've met them sometime."

"Maybe so." John Titus' eyes closed for a minute. "Dundee, go fetch my foreman, Strother James. We got plans to make."

Millie McCown had fashioned a wooden cross and placed it at the grave. The minister John Titus had brought read words from the Bible. A pale Tobe Crane stood bareheaded in the sun, his good hand clasped with Millie's. Dundee noticed, and regret touched him, but it was covered over by the regret he felt as he watched old John Titus crush his hat in his hands, looking down at the mound of earth which was all he would ever again see of his son.

Around the grave stood some thirty men, each wearing a pistol, each holding a horse that carried a full supply of ammunition in bulging saddlebags. Some wore badges that John Titus had browbeaten the sheriff into passing out as he deputized the lot of them. There hadn't been nearly enough badges to go around. Dundee had not chosen to wear one, for somehow he felt ill at ease that close to a star. The legal authority was vested in the badges. The practical authority they all carried in their holsters, and in the saddle scabbards that bristled with carbines and shotguns.

The minister finished his prayer. The cowboys waited awkwardly for John Titus to put his hat on, then they followed suit, their attention focused on the old man. John Titus shook hands with the minister. "Thanks, preacher. Now I reckon you better be heading back, for the Lord's work here is done. What comes next is the devil's own."

The minister was a thin old man of about Titus' age, badly used up by the rigors of the range country. He said: "I'd rather stand by you, John. I think you'll have need of me before it's done."

But John Titus wouldn't let him.

Tobe Crane took his good hand from Millie's grasp and held it out toward John Titus. "I'll be going with you."

The old man glanced at the bound arm. "Much obliged, boy, but you'd best stay here and mend. I won't forget that you got them wounds helping Son."

"He was my friend. That's why I'm going with you."

Dundee broke in. "You won't be able to keep up, Tobe."

"I'll keep up. You won't have to slow down none for me."

Dundee was about to tell Tobe again that he couldn't go, but John Titus cut him off. "Then, boy, you come on along." The old man turned his attention to the girl. "Much obliged to you and your family, miss, for everything you done. I won't forget it."

Warren McCown stood to one side, watching but not quite a part of it. Titus said to him: "What I told your sister, I meant. If ever there's something I can do for you. . . ."

Warren shook his head. "We'll do all right."

Titus turned to Dundee and his thirty or so men. "Boys, we got us a job to do."

Ahead of them, atop a gentle slope that led down toward a narrow creek, sat a cabin of liveoak logs, with a rude lean-to of cedar and a set of brush corrals rambling away lazily toward the hill. Three horses were staked on green grass, their ropes long enough to allow them to go down to the creek for water. In front of the cabin three saddles lay dumped on the ground, blankets flopped across them.

Three saddles, three men, Dundee thought.

When they had left the McCown place, John Titus had said, "Lead out, Dundee." Dundee hadn't realized the old man meant for him to take command. Now as they looked down on the cabin, old Titus said, "What you planning to do, Dundee?"

"I was planning on taking orders."

"I was planning on you giving them."

Dundee's jaw dropped. "I'm no Ranger or general or nothing like that. I been a cowboy all my life."

"You're drawing a right smart more than cowboy pay. I'm counting on you to earn it." With that, the old man just pulled back and checked it to him.

Dundee chewed a little, though there was nothing in his mouth for him to chew on. What smattering of knowledge he had about gunfighting was of a personal nature, man to man. It didn't cover military tactics. What's more, the men with him were cowboys for the most part, not gunhands, though Titus' foreman Strother James had managed to round up a few men who had had experience either packing a star or avoiding one; it would be hard to tell which.

Dundee figured he would have to put most of his hope in those, and in the caprices of Lady Luck, who on occasion had been known to spit in his eye.

He made a sweeping motion with his arm, signaling for a surround. He sat on the bay horse and watched while the men spread out and around the cabin, shutting off any chance for escape by the men inside. Right away he saw his first mistake. The way the posse had tightened the ring, there was no way for anyone to shoot without taking a chance of hitting one of his own men. Dundee signaled for the riders on the opposite side to move up the hill, out of the line of fire.

This was a soldiering job, and for a moment he wished he were old enough to have been in the war, so he would be sure what he was up to. But hell, he would be old and gray now, and fighting off the rheumatism.

The cabin door opened. A bareheaded man stepped out in red underwear, denim britches and long-eared boots. He walked along with head down, whistling. At the woodpile he picked up a chunk of mesquite and placed it across the chopping block. When the ax fell, Dundee started his bay forward, wondering how long it would be before the posse was seen. The woodchopper was so preoccupied, Dundee got close enough that he could chunk a rock at him. These renegades had stolen cattle here so long with absolute impunity there was no reason to suspect the puckerstring was about to draw shut.

The ax stopped its swing above the chopper's head. He gaped at Dundee, then let his gaze drift slowly to the other riders spread out across the flat. He stood that way for long seconds, the ax raised, his mouth and eyes wide. Of a sudden he flung the ax behind him and turned to run for the shack.

"Stop!" Dundee called. The man halted in midstride. Dundee let his voice drop a little. "You'd never make the door. If you don't want some new holes opened up in you, better turn around here and see how high you can raise them hands."

The rustler turned slowly, shaking. Dundee stepped down and handed the reins to the angular old brushpopper Strother James. He slapped the palms of his hands against the outlaw's pockets and down against his boottops.

"No gun. Wouldn't of been no use to you anyway. I take it there's still two men in the shack."

The outlaw swallowed, his stubbled neck quivering. He tried to speak, but nothing came out. He nodded instead, his eyes darting from one rider to another, frightened as a rabbit's. Dundee guessed he was looking at the ropes on their saddles.

"Do what I tell you and maybe you won't have to try

one of them on for size," Dundee said. "You call to your friends in there and tell them to come on out. Tell them we got them hemmed in tighter than Maggie's britches."

For a minute he was afraid the outlaw was going to be of no use to him, for the man was so scared that his voice wouldn't function. "Give her another try," Dundee said firmly.

The outlaw cupped his hands around his mouth. "Jake! Hawk! They got us! You better come out!"

Dundee kept the outlaw between him and the cabin. He drew his pistol and stood waiting, his heart quickening. He saw motion at a window. A man stepped out of the door, crouching warily, rifle in his hand. He looked at the ring of horsemen and realized he had made a mistake. "Arnie, what's going on out here?"

Dundee said, "Drop the rifle and walk this way."

The outlaw still crouched, his head turning slowly as he counted the men who waited for his decision.

He made the wrong one. He decided to try for the cabin. Dundee leveled his pistol but never squeezed the trigger. A rifle roared in old John Titus' hands, and half a dozen more shots exploded in the space of a second or two. Dundee could see the puffs of dust as the bullets struck, twisting the outlaw, one way, slamming him another. The rifle flew out of the man's grasp. He fell without a whimper, cut to pieces.

Dundee heard the outlaw in front of him whisper "God!" and sink to his knees. The horses danced in fear at the sudden fusillade, smoke rising from half a dozen guns. He heard excited shouts from men who hadn't been able to see, wanting to know what was going on.

Dundee caught his breath. "You still got one friend in there. If he's any friend atall, you better tell him to come out with his hands up."

Arnie found his voice this time. "Jake, Hawk's dead. They got him. You come on out while you still can."

The door opened cautiously. Dundee saw the barrel of a rifle and leveled his pistol on it. The rifle was thrown onto the ground. The door opened wider and a man swayed out, his arms held straight up. "Don't shoot! Don't nobody shoot!"

Dundee motioned him forward. The men rode in closer, covering the outlaws with their rifles and shotguns and six-shooters. Dundee turned and stared a moment at all the hardware, and he felt almost as nervous as these cowthieves. That much artillery in the hands of a bunch of cowboys was enough to make a man break out into a cold sweat. "You boys be careful with them guns. We want to be damn choosy who we kill."

John Titus edged his horse forward. He leaned on his saddlehorn and stared down at the two cowthieves, his eyes hard as steel. "Dundee, you reckon these two could've done it? You reckon they killed Son?"

Dundee knew he had to be careful how he answered, for the old man's fingers inched down to touch his rope. "These two ain't no more likely than anybody else." Dundee could see the temper in the eyes of the men around him. If old Titus said the word, they'd hang these two from the nearest liveoak. Dundee held his breath. That kind of a show wasn't what he had come for.

Titus stared a long time before he said: "Tie them on their horses. We'll take them with us to the next place."

Strother James fingered his gray-laced beard, then pointed to the dead man. "What about him?"

"What *about* him? Leave him there."

Pistol in hand, Dundee approached the shack. He was reasonably sure the three men were all who had been here, but in a situation like this the man who took things for granted might not be around to celebrate next Christmas. He kicked the door open and leaped inside. A quick glance told him he was by himself. He slipped the pistol back into its holster. Seeing a lantern hanging from the ceiling, he took it and emptied the kerosene along the walls. In a corner he found a coal oil can that felt as if it were half full. He poured fuel onto the outside walls, then stepped back and struck a match on the sole of his boot. He flipped it into a patch of dry grass at the base of the wall. The flame grabbed the kerosene and raced up toward the roof, crackling. Dundee heard the horses snort in fear of the fire.

The outlaw named Arnie said plaintively, "I got a little money hid in there."

Dundee watched the flames lick across the wall and find their way into the cabin, the dark smoke aboil. "You *had* a little money in there," he corrected.

They moved fast and struck hard, over the hills, up the valleys, following Dundee's map, picking up one thief's camp and then another, leaving behind them smoke and flame. During that blazing afternoon one more outlaw showed the poor judgment to come out with rifle firing, and he stayed there on the spot where he had fallen, dead before his dropped weapon ever struck the ground.

Through it all, old John Titus never let age cause him to falter or drop behind. He moved in silence, his gaunt face like darkened rawhide dried on a stretching frame. He watched the gradually-increasing string of prisoners brought along on their own horses, hands thong-tied to saddlehorns. Titus had nothing to say until after the fourth camp had been taken. He edged his horse against Dundee's.

"These are little fish," he said solemnly. "I want the big one."

"Old Roan? He'll be harder to take. While we're trying, a lot of the others will slip out of the country."

"Let them. It's Roan I want. Wherever we find Roan, we'll likely find the man who killed Son."

Dundee shrugged. He had rather have concentrated on the easy ones, as much to sharpen up this inexperienced posse as anything else. It was one thing to ride into a two-bit rustler camp and flush out one, two or three miserable cowthieves. It might be entirely something else to beard the lion in his own den.

Titus said: "You know where Roan has his headquarters, don't you? You showed it on your map."

"I know where it is. I just wasn't too anxious to see it yet."

"*I'm* anxious."

So they rode. Sundown caught them still many miles from Runaway, but Dundee figured that might be a good thing. The darkness would help hide their movements.

He didn't know how much surprise there might still be. They had moved swiftly today, and so far as he knew, nobody had gone through the net. But it would be hard to know for sure. Somebody might have come over a hilltop and spotted them without himself being seen. If so, he probably wouldn't let his shirttail touch him till he reached Roan Hardesty.

"Pull them prisoners in tight," he ordered. "We can't let a one of them get away. Tie all their horses onto one rope and lead them."

Far into the night they rode, Dundee always a little ahead, feeling out the way in the near darkness. There was a trail, but he chose not to follow it. They cut across the hills, climbing wherever he could find a way through, easing down off the slopes, splashing through the moon-trapping creeks that shimmered in the lazy valleys.

He had never been down to Roan Hardesty's headquarters, but he had sat on top of a hill and watched it through the glass most of one afternoon, getting the hang of it. Roan's taste in a ranch layout was much the same as his taste in whisky: rawness was no detriment so long as the thing fitted its purpose. The old reprobate lived in a small log house just far enough up from the creekbank that he wouldn't have to flee the floodwater. He evidently didn't want to tote water any farther than absolutely necessary. His barn—such as it was—had been built close to the house, too. Sanitation wasn't as much worry to him as the length of the walk from where he had to turn his horse loose.

Roan's men—the ones he kept around him all the time—stayed in a long, low rock structure with a brush-and-mud roof. Far as Dundee had been able to tell, Roan lived in the log house all by himself, though he had had some female company there the afternoon Dundee had spied from afar. Plain house, raw whisky and a painted woman. A man should never get so rich but what he still enjoyed the simple pleasures, Dundee had told himself.

For a while he feared he was lost in the night, but at last he found the hill where he had sat that time before. The men came up around him and let their horses rest. The dim moonlight barely showed the outlines of the buildings down there.

John Titus said, "Is that where he's at?"

"Well, it's where he lives. He spends a lot of time in Runaway. The only light I can see is a lamp in the bunkhouse. Roan's place is dark."

"You reckon he found out about us and ran?"

"Maybe. Or he could be in town playing poker. Or, he could be laying in there asleep. I expect he sleeps a right smart, his age and all." Dundee frowned. "You need some rest yourself, Mister Titus. You been going awful strong."

"I'll rest when the job is done. There won't be much left for me to work for, when this is over. Son is gone."

Dundee didn't know how to answer that, so he didn't try. He had a notion that when the old man's initial grief passed, he'd be back in harness as strong as ever. Work was what kept a man like him going. Dundee said: "We'll *all* get some rest. If they *have* heard we're in the country, they could be waiting there somewhere trying to catch us in the dark. We'd best wait till daylight. But we'll move down closer and put a surround on them. That way there can't nobody slip in, or nobody slip out."

Since he seemed to be the one giving orders, Dundee told the men not to light any cigarettes through the night. That would be a giveaway.

Later a weary Tobe Crane sat beside Dundee where they could look down on the dark shape of the buildings. Crane had kept his word. Weak though he was, he hadn't fallen behind a single time.

Before long Dundee started seeing matches flare in the night, one, two . . . then five and six. He swore. "Looky there. Them matches can be seen for miles. I told them boy. . . ."

"A nervous man is bound and bedamned to smoke. And this is a nervous bunch."

Dundee grunted. "Ever so often I think about all them shooting irons in the hands of cowpunchers, and I get a mite nervous myself."

"You got a plan how we're going to take that place?"

"I ain't no general. All I know to do is just ride down there and take over."

"Looks awful risky."

"Everything we've done has been risky."

Dundee didn't intend to, but he dropped off to sleep. The first thing he heard was a rooster crowing somewhere down at the ranch headquarters. He yawned and glanced eastward, where dawn was sending up the first faint promise of color.

Tobe's eyes flickered in surprise when the rooster crowed again. "Is that what it sounds like?"

Dundee nodded. Tobe said: "I wouldn't picture Roan Hardesty as being the type to keep a bunch of chickens around."

Dundee smiled. There *was* something awfully domestic about a set of clucking hens.

Tobe said: "Maybe he enjoys wringing necks."

"More likely he just favors eggs. Old men get contrary about what they eat, and *tough* old men can get *awful* contrary."

Dundee could see the cowboys stirring around, and he knew they hadn't slept much, most of them. From the dark pockets under Tobe's eyes, Dundee could tell *he* hadn't. Tobe said: "I could sure stand a cup of hot coffee."

"We'll cook breakfast on old Roan's stove."

He sent a cowboy to carry word to all the men who encircled Blue Roan's layout: they would move in fifteen minutes. Everybody was to watch Dundee. When he broke into the open, they were all to ride fast and try to get as close as they could. He took out his watch and marked the time. He had gone without a cigarette all night. He had followed his own orders, even if nobody else had. Now in the coming daylight he guessed it wouldn't hurt to light one. He turned his back to the houses, though, and hid the flare with his body till he shook the match out. Most of the fifteen minutes were up when the cowboy came back.

Dundee dropped his cigarette on the ground, saddled his horse and checked his saddlegun. "Everybody here ready?"

Old John Titus sat waiting. Dundee couldn't tell whether he had slept or not; he doubted it. In fact, he doubted that

Titus had really known sound sleep since Dundee had brought him word about Son. Dark shadows framed the eyes that seemed drawn back into the stony face. But there was an incandescence to those eyes, a fire that Dundee feared it might take a lot of blood to quench.

"I seen everybody," he said. "They'll be looking for you."

The saddlegun in his hand, ready for use, Dundee swung up. He glanced around to be sure the others were mounted, then said, "Let's go amongst them."

He touched the bay's ribs firmly with the spurs and brought the horse into a long trot down the slope. When he hit the flat terrain, he spurred into a hard lope. Around him he could see the other riders closing in, following his lead. A few shouted like Comanches, and he thought that was a foolish thing to do.

The horse's long stride reached out and gathered in the yards. The outbuildings seemed to rush headlong toward him, and he expected any second the puffs of smoke, the crackle of gunfire.

He could see the windows now, and count the panes; they were getting that close, the horses running full tilt, the hoofs drumming, the dust lifting in plumes as they crossed the grassless roundup grounds near the corrals. *Any second now they'll commence shooting at us.*

He watched the windows, for that was where the firing would come from, most likely.

It didn't start.

Maybe they're waiting for us to get so close they can't miss. They'll wait for us to poke our faces in those windows and then they'll blow our heads off. This is a damn-fool way to do it anyhow. A smart man would've sneaked us in there like a bunch of Indians.

He was into the yard now, not a hundred feet from Blue Roan's log house. Dundee realized he was holding his breath, his lungs afire. The last few feet his heart was beating so hard he thought he could hear it, but it was only the hoofs.

Then he was at the house itself. He swung his leg over the bay's hips before the horse slid to a stop. Dundee jumped free and lit running, expecting a blast from the nearest window. He flattened against rough logs, breathing hard. He realized that not a shot had been fired.

He didn't wait to puzzle it out. He ran for the door, kicked it open with one hard thrust of his foot and leaped inside, hands tight on the carbine, ready to fire at the first thing that moved.

Nothing did. Dundee crouched, his chest heaving, his confused gaze sweeping the room.

Not a soul here. Just empty tin cans and dirty dishes, a whisky bottle on the floor; an unmade bed in a corner, a single dark stocking lying on the blankets, the kind the wheeligo girls wore in the saloons. Dundee examined the messed-up plates and found the food had dried. Nobody had eaten here since sometime yesterday.

He whirled at the sound of a footstep on the board floor. He lowered the carbine as he saw Tobe Crane. Crane's voice was heavy with disappointment. "There's nobody here."

"Maybe the bunkhouse."

Tobe shook his head. "Boys already been there. There was a lamp on the table, the coal oil all used up and the chimney burned black as pitch. They fooled us, Dundee. They must of knowed we was coming. Looks like they slipped away and left that lamp to fool us."

Stepping outside, Dundee watched the cowboys search the barn, the corrals. He let his gaze drift to the hill from which they had started.

Tobe Crane was looking the same way. "Maybe it's a good thing there wasn't anybody here. We'd of made perfect targets."

"I never claimed to be no West Point wonder. Leading green cowpunchers into a gunfight ain't my bowl of *chili* in the first place."

Tobe said: "Maybe we ought to've known we couldn't fool an old fox like Roan. He's got eyes in the back of his head, and maybe in his rump." He paused, studying. "Maybe old Roan took to the tulies."

"It'd take more than this bunch of cow nurses to scare Roan Hardesty out of a place like this, and away from a fortune in burnt cattle. I expect he took out for Runaway, where he'd have extra men, and maybe a better place to fight."

Old John Titus silently stared at Dundee, the disappointment keen in his pinched eyes.

Dundee said: "Mister Titus, we better send for more help. If Roan has holed up in Runaway—and I figure he has—there ain't enough of us to root him out. These cowboys of yours have got their hearts in the right place, but very little else."

The old man nodded slowly. "That's already took care of. Before we left, I got word out to other ranches around us . . . told them what we was fixing to do. I told them to send men to Runaway. This is *their* fight, too."

"More cowboys? What we need is Rangers."

"I waited till the very last to send word to the Rangers. I didn't want them getting in our way. They get kind of sticky about rules." The old man made a sweep with his arm. "Let's burn it all. Then we'll get on down to Runaway."

XII

Dundee had been on this hill overlooking Runaway so many times that he had just about all of the town memorized. He thought by now he knew the position of every building, every outdoor convenience, every rainbarrel. Looking down, he decided everything was in its proper place. Nothing moved, not even a jackrabbit.

He sensed Tobe Crane sitting on his horse beside him. Dundee said, "Well, they're down there all right, just waiting for us."

"How do you know? I don't see a thing."

"That's how you can tell."

John Titus halted beside Dundee, taking his first real look at Runaway. Dundee could see the old man's jaw harden. "So that's the place. That's the rattlesnake den that killed my boy."

Dundee nodded. "That's Runaway."

Titus' voice was like two strands of barbed wire rubbed together. "It won't be there when we leave."

"They're ready for us," Dundee said. "We ain't got the manpower just to ride in and take over. They'd cut us down like weeds. Maybe we ought to leave Runaway alone. There's a heap of little rustler camps we could handle instead. With them gone, Runaway would wither anyhow."

"We didn't come to catch a handful of rats. We come to wipe out the nest," Titus said.

Dundee rubbed his jaw. "It's a hell of a big nest."

"We come to take it."

Dundee turned in the saddle and looked back over the cowboys. Thirty of them he had, plus a wounded Tobe Crane and a bitter old man whose hatred was far steadier than his gnarled hand. "It won't come cheap."

"I'll pay the price. You afraid, Dundee?"

Dundee frowned. "It ain't like being in church."

"They can be taken. We got enough men to surround the town and keep anybody from getting out. Sooner or later they'll have to give up."

"They probably got enough food to carry them awhile. I know they got lots of whisky."

"You'll see, Dundee. They'll break down. They'll get nervous waiting, and sooner or later they'll try to bust out. We'll be here, and we'll be ready."

"It'll scatter us pretty thin, trying to surround the whole town."

"When the will is strong enough. . . ."

Dundee would admit that the will of these cowboys was plenty strong. If only they had the aim to go with it. . . . "We'll try it your way, Mister Titus."

"You're damn right you will."

Along the way Dundee had tried to make a study of the

men and pick out the best fighting prospects. Two or three of them, he judged, could as well be down there in Runaway as up here waiting to lay siege to it. But so long as they were in on it, he was glad they were on his side instead of against him. He started down off the hill and began a wide circle of the town, dropping off a man here, a man there, at fairly regular intervals where there was cover. About every third or fourth place he dropped one of the men he thought might be better than average with a gun. He placed the men in a wide semi-circle, for the bluff itself effectively sealed off that side of the town.

"If they decide to try a break," he told the men, "they'll go for what they figure is the weakest spot in our line. One man won't be much hindrance to them. If you see trouble, burn leather getting there. The man on that spot will need all the help he can get."

He didn't really expect any such break. The outlaws probably felt a strong confidence in their superiority over a little bunch of green cowboys. If they'd wanted to leave Runaway, they would have done it before this posse got here.

The men all placed, he paused at the foot of the hill and looked at the town. Curiosity began to nettle him. How close *could* they get in there? The wagonyard caught his eye. It struck him that if the wind blew hard enough, and if a man could get to that barn and drop a match into dry hay, fire might spread down the street, touching off first one building, then the next. It was a narrow-odds bet, but he'd taken risks ever since he'd left home as a kid, gambling that he wouldn't starve to death. He'd almost lost *that* bet.

He touched a spur to the horse's ribs and decided to see just how far he could get.

He quickly found out. Dundee saw the flash of a rifle and heard a bullet ricochet off the rocks with a vicious whine. He whirled and spurred for the hill. His curiosity was satisfied.

John Titus and Tobe Crane waited on top of the hill. Tobe was not physically able to contribute much; it amazed Dundee that he'd gotten this far without dropping from exhaustion. And he knew he couldn't count on the old man for much action. He said, "Well, sir, I reckon you can see that they've dug into there like lice in a buffalo robe."

Titus' expression never altered. "They can't stay forever."

Presently Dundee's eye was caught by movement in the street, then at the wagonyard. A man rode out of the corral with a rifle in his hand, waving a white cloth tied to the end of it. He moved toward the hill.

John Titus' eyes went wide as spur rowels. "They're giving up."

Dundee said: "Not hardly, not when they got most of the chips on their end of the table. I expect they want to palaver. I'll go down and see what it's all about."

Tobe Crane warned: "You watch them, Dundee. It'd tickle them to see you dead."

"I'll watch. That idea don't appeal to me."

He took his time, his gaze never straying far from the horseman who held the rifle and the white cloth. It occurred to Dundee that the rifle was probably loaded, just in case. His lips dry, his nerves wound tight as a watchspring, he strongly considered drawing his carbine and making sure it was loaded too. But he resisted.

He recognized Jason Karnes. Now he *knew* that rifle was loaded.

He stopped and let the be-stubbled Karnes travel the last few lengths to meet him. Dundee noticed how the man's leg was held out stiffly away from the saddle. *A little souvenir I gave him.* They stared cold-eyed at each other a minute before Dundee said, "I bet that was *you* who shot at me a little while ago."

Karnes nodded. "It was."

"I'm pleased to find your aim ain't improved much."

"It'll get better. I got me a crippled leg now. They say when a man loses one thing, he gains someplace else. I'm counting on a better shooting eye."

"You ought to've counted on your horse-picking eye and cut you out a fast one to get you away from here. There's an old man up yonder on that hill who's come to see blood."

"He's still on the hill, though. And that's as far as he's

going to get. Except under a flag of truce. That's what Roan sent me for. He wants to parley with old man Titus.''

"I'll ask him.''

"Roan says tell the old man not to bring a gun, and Roan won't bring his either.''

Dundee's eyes narrowed. "And maybe ride into a trap? No thanks. The old man may come without a gun, but *I* won't. I'll come along to be sure there don't nothing happen to him.''

"Fair enough. And I'll be here to take care of old Roan case one of your bunch gets a foolish notion.''

Karnes slowly turned his horse around and started back toward town. He shifted his body in the saddle so he could watch Dundee over his shoulder.

Dundee wasn't even that trustful. He waited until the distance between them had stretched to a good fifty yards before he brought his bay around. He carried the message back up the hill.

John Titus clenched tough fists. "I got nothing to talk to Roan about.''

"You say you figure on staying here and starving them out if you have to. Maybe you could convince him of that.''

"I won't make him no promises I don't intend to keep. And I know what I plan to do with Roan when I get my hands on him.''

So did Dundee. The thought had gnawed on him for a long time. "It won't hurt to go down and talk.''

He prevailed on John Titus to leave his pistol and his saddlegun with Tobe at the top of the hill. They started down together. In town, a long way off, Dundee could see two horsemen leave the corral and start toward them. Jason Karnes was still riding the same stocking-legged black he had been on a little while ago. The other figure was the unmistakably blocky one of Roan Hardesty, riding that dappled gray he favored so much.

Dundee asked John Titus, "How long since you've seen Blue Roan?''

Titus thoughtfully shook his head. "Many and many a year.''

"You may not know him, then."

"I'll know him. I'd know his hide in a tanyard."

A tiny group of liveoaks clustered below the hill. There Dundee and John Titus stopped to wait, for it was about the halfway point. Dundee had brought his saddlegun across his lap now, ready. He noted that Jason Karnes had done the same.

Roan Hardesty didn't rein up until his horse was touching necks with that of John Titus. The blue splotches on his face stood out like the dapple marks on his horse. His eyes were soft with an offering of friendship. "It's been a long time, John." He held out his right hand.

John Titus let his own hands remain at his sides. His eyes were cold as December and seemed to freeze onto Roan Hardesty. He made no effort to reply.

Roan slowly drew back his hand and rubbed it nervously on his huge leg. He looked down a moment, framing his words as if each might fall back and crush him. "John, I felt real bad about your boy. Maybe Dundee has told you: I give orders there wasn't nobody to kill him. I've turned this town upside down, trying to find out who it was went against my orders. Nobody'll own up to it." He paused, waiting for a reaction that didn't come. "I swear to you, John, if I knowed who it was, I'd kill him myself."

John Titus' throat showed a tremor. "I come to see you die, Roan."

The aging outlaw slumped in the saddle. "We was friends for a long time, John. We warred together, remember? We rode the brush together. We seen the elephant and heard the owl hoot."

"I got a boy dead now, Roan."

"John, I've took a lot of your cows; Lord, I wouldn't deny that. But I never took your son. I never had no intention for harm to come to him."

Titus repeated, quieter this time, "I come to see you die."

The silence between them then was long and heavy. They stared at each other, the outlaw's eyes regretful, Titus' eyes cold and grim. It was Roan who finally spoke. "Well, John, I've said all I can. I'm sorry the way it all happened. We was friends a long time. But if this is where friendship has to end, so be it. You can't take our town, not with what you got here. You'd never even get into the street.''

"We got you all bottled up. All we got to do now is outlast you. I'll stay all summer if I have to, and into the fall.''

Roan Hardesty looked around him, trying to pick out the places where Dundee had stationed the men. "What you got, John? Twenty-five men? Thirty? And just cowboys at that." His eyes narrowed. "I'll tell you something you didn't know. I got friends scattered all over them hills. I sent word last night to the forks of the creek. When they all get here, it'll look like the Confederate army. They'll run over your bunch like wild studs over pet ponies.''

Dundee stiffened. He hoped it wouldn't show. This was one thing he hadn't considered, that Hardesty might get reinforcements in substantial numbers.

Titus said tightly: "We'll take care of ourselves, Roan. Tell your men that every time one of them sticks his head out, somebody's going to take a shot at him. They'll get almighty tired of dodging every time they need a bucket of water or a sack of beans.''

Roan's splotchy face was clouded now with trouble. "I'll tell them, John." He started to turn away but paused. "There's some women down in town, and a few men that got no part in this. Ain't fair to risk getting them hurt. I'd like to send them out, John.''

"Send them, then. We got no war on against women.''

Dundee watched John Titus' face as Roan Hardesty slowly rode back toward town. If a momentary softness showed here, it was quickly covered by a steely determination.

Dundee offered: "I think he's telling you the truth, Mister Titus. I don't think he knows who killed Son.''

Titus was silent.

In a little while a horseman appeared outside the barn, a white cloth tied to a long stick. He rode into the clear, stopped and waved the cloth from side to side so everyone could see it. Then he turned in the saddle. Out from the corrals came two buckboards and a wagon, trailed by a second horseman. Even at the distance Dundee could see the ribbons and streamers and colored dresses.

"The women," he said. "They're coming out."

Titus' brow furrowed. "No children?"

"This ain't exactly a family town."

The front rider, carrying the white cloth, was the wagonyard operator. Behind him, in the buckboard, Dundee could recognize Katy Long. Driving was the little bartender Cricket. As they came up even with Dundee, Katy motioned for Cricket to stop. She looked Dundee straight in the eye, and he thought she might be laughing a little. "See, Dundee? I told you you'd be back."

"And I told you to sell that saloon. Did you?"

"Nobody made me an offer."

"A pity."

Any smile she might have had was suddenly gone. "You don't really think you can take that town, do you? With *that* bunch of men?"

"Titus says we'll take it. So, we'll take it."

"Roan Hardesty says you won't. He doesn't make many mistakes."

"He's made one."

The wagonyard operator got as close to Dundee as he could. "Friend, I got a valuable piece of property down there. I've always tried to treat you square."

"Like double-charging me for hay?"

"I'm sorry we had a misunderstanding over that." He reached in his pocket and came up with a silver coin. "Here, I'd like to pay you back."

"Keep it. When this is over, that may be all you got left."

Some of the women were protesting angrily, while others just sat and looked frightened. A couple tried to flirt with Dundee. He waved them on. The horseman who came along behind the wagons was a middle-aged, portly gent Dundee hadn't seen before. "Mister Dundee, my name is Smith, and I'm a legitimate businessman. I own the mercantile down there." He offered his hand, but Dundee ignored it. Smith went on: "I have a considerable investment. What you're doing here is jeopardizing my property. I'd like to see it stopped, immediately.''

"Oh, you would?"

"I would dislike having to protest to the state authorities, but I will if I must. You have no right to stand in the way of an honest businessman and disrupt his trade.''

Dundee turned in the saddle and pointed east. "Well, now, you just go right ahead and protest if you want to. About two days' hard ride in that direction will get you to Austin. Three days if that saddle makes your rump sore.''

He hoped the women would go on, but they didn't. They moved a little way down the road and proceeded to set up camp. Dundee thought about all those women, and all those cowboys. You couldn't keep up much of a siege when half your men weren't on duty. He said a few choice words under his breath, swung onto the bay and trotted down to where the women were struggling to get up a couple of big tents. He noted that Katy Long was not among them, a point which brought him considerable satisfaction.

"You can just take that thing down and put it back in the wagon," he hollered. "You're not going to use it here."

The big red-headed woman he had had a run-in with before came stalking forward like an angry she-bear, her hands on her hips. Dundee wouldn't have been much surprised if she had breathed fire at him. She didn't, but her breath was bad enough. "Who the hell says so?"

"Me."

She looked back over her shoulder. The women had the tent just about set up. "Now, Mister Tall, Dark and Ugly, what do you intend to do about it? Are you low-down enough to shoot a woman? You'd have to, you know, before we'd take that tent down."

Dundee tried to hold his rising temper. "I'd ask you real polite."

"Well, we won't take it down. So what do you do now?"

Dundee said, "Then *I'll* take it down."

He lifted his hornstring and freed his rope. He shook out a loop and spurred the bay into a brisk trot, nearly bumping the redhead before she could jump aside, cursing. He swung the loop while the women ran screaming. He dropped it over the top of the tent, jerked out the slack, dallied the rope around the horn and squalled a cowboy yell as he spurred the bay into a run. The tent stakes flipped out of the ground, and the tent came sailing after him. The horses took a wild-eyed look at the flying apparition and stampeded. The wagon bounced behind them, scattering clothes and camp goods for two hundred yards up the trail.

Dundee stopped and freed his rope. Recoiling it, he rode back into a circle of shaken, angry women. His gaze fastened on the redhead. "Like I was saying, you ain't stopping here. I'll go fetch your team back, and you'll be going on your way."

He rode up the trail to where the team had finally stopped. At the side of the road, Katy Long had halted her buckboard and had witnessed the excitement from afar. Now she watched grinning as Dundee approached. "You play rough, Dundee."

"Them women got no business here. They'd just be a temptation to the men."

"Am I included?"

"You're not like them others. But you'd be a temptation to *me*."

"Well, thanks for that."

The bartender Cricket helped him take the wagon back. Dundee didn't leave till he saw the women on their way. Even then he knew they wouldn't travel far. He had seen cows that would move only so long as a horseman pushed them. When he stopped pushing, they would stop moving. Dundee knew the women would move on a mile or two, then stop again, confident Roan's bunch would win and they could go back to Runaway.

At least they would be out from under foot.

At the hill, he watched with John Titus and Tobe Crane as a man started across the street from one saloon toward another. Half a dozen rifles rattled from vantage points around town, including a couple on top of the cliff. Dust kicked up in half a dozen places. The man turned and trotted briskly back where he had come from.

"Not very good shots, are they?" Dundee said.

"They try," Titus replied defensively.

"Trying ain't going to be enough."

In retaliation, rifles set up a racket down in town, Hardesty's men trying to find the places where the cowboys were spotted. So far as Dundee could tell, their aim wasn't a lot better. "Looks to me like a Mexican standoff. We can't go in, and they can't go out."

"We can wait," said Titus. "Time is on our side."

Dundee frowned. "I don't know. I got the feeling old Roan didn't lie about having more men on the way. I tell you, Mister Titus, if there's many of them they can circle our outfit and pick off them boys one at a time. It'd be like shooting ducks in a tank."

"I told you, Dundee, I sent for more help too."

"You didn't get no promises, did you?"

Titus didn't answer.

Through the long afternoon they sat impatiently watching, waiting, Dundee trying a little mumblepeg, then whittling sticks down to a pile of white shavings, whistling some half-forgotten tune till it felt as if his lips would crack. The old man huddled most of the time like some wounded eagle, his gaze fastened on the town. Tobe Crane paced till he got tired, sat awhile, arose and paced some more. It finally got on Dundee's nerves.

"You're supposed to be recuperating. Sit down and get still."

"Walking don't bother me."

"It bothers *me*. Sit down."

Tobe Crane did as he was told, but he took his time, as if to show that if the idea didn't suit him he wouldn't have done it. Dundee softened a little. "I didn't much cotton to you coming along in the first place. You don't take care of yourself, Millie's liable to blame me. She's invested a lot of work in getting you on your feet."

Tobe Crane stared at the ground. "Yes, she has."

Dundee studied the cowboy, his eyes narrowed in speculation. "She's a real pretty girl. A man could lose his head over her," he said.

Crane said, "She seemed to think a great deal of you, Dundee."

Dundee winced. From somewhere came a touch of pain. "I'll admit, I've done a heap of thinking . . . wonder if ever I could make myself settle down and try to build a home for a girl like that."

Crane glanced at him a second and looked away. "You still thinking about it?"

"Some."

"Made up your mind?"

"Not yet. I'm afraid I know other people better than I know myself."

"Are you sure you know Millie?"

"I think so."

Tobe Crane pushed to his feet again and stared wistful-eyed down the valley. "I hope you don't figure her wrong."

XIII

They had salvaged a chuckwagon from Roan Hardesty's place before they put it to the torch. Now a couple of the men cooked supper, and the cowboys rode in a few at a time to eat. Dundee tried, but he couldn't stir up much appetite, looking down upon that town. They weren't any closer to it now than they had been this morning. He couldn't help thinking that Roan's reinforcements might show up, and then it would be hell among the yearlings.

The breeze came up with twilight, a breeze out of the south. Dundee got to mulling again the idea that had occurred to him during the day . . . setting fire to the town and forcing the renegades out. He hadn't gotten past the turnrow the first time, but that had been daylight. With luck a man might sneak through in the dark.

He told the old man about the notion, and Titus seemed receptive. He would accept anything right now except retreat. Tobe Crane said, "I'll go down there with you, Dundee."

"You stay here. You ain't got the strength," Dundee said.

"That's what you thought before. I'll go with you."

Dundee didn't argue any further. Tobe Crane was a grown man and able to make his own mind up . . . even if now and then he did seem to have more guts than sense. They circled southward, visiting all the posts to tell the men what they were up to.

"I wouldn't want to get the job done and then be shot by our own bunch," Dundee said. "That'd be a real joke on us."

From the south Dundee remembered a clump of liveoaks about halfway between their outposts and the first outbuildings of the town. Saddlegun across his lap, he slow-walked the bay in that direction, hoping to get done before the moon came up. Dundee could sense Tobe Crane's nervousness. Tobe had punched cows all his life. He'd probably never been shot at till the first time he came to Runaway.

"Easy, boy," Dundee whispered. "If they spot us, be ready to leave here like a Jeff Davis cannonball."

They made the trees, somewhat to Dundee's surprise. He tied the bay. "If we get in a jam, Tobe, you run like the devil. Don't wait on me. It's every man for himself."

Dundee moved out from the trees in a crouch, saddlegun cradled in his arm. Because of his wound, Tobe carried only a six-shooter, and Dundee doubted he could hit his own hat with it. But it was reassuring to have company.

The first building they reached was a cowshed, with lots of dry hay in it. That, Dundee figured, would burn easily. The breeze was still out of the south, and it stood a good chance of carrying the fire through the summer-dried grass on into the rest of town. But the closer he could get to start his fire, the better the odds. He decided to try next for an empty-looking log shack. He bent low and sprinted across a short clearing. Flattening himself against the logs, he waited for any sign that he had been seen. When none came, he motioned for Tobe.

They'd made it this far. Maybe they could do even better. The next building was the frame house where he had found Son Titus whiling time away with the girl Lutie. He thought it ought to burn with a jolly blaze. He eased out to make a try for it. He had gone three long strides when a voice came from one of the open windows. "What you doing out there?"

Dundee's heart leaped, but he decided to brazen it on through. "Looking for a bottle. You got an extra one?"

"No. You go find your own."

Dundee let out a long-held breath. Well, he'd found out how far he could go. He retreated to the shack and Tobe Crane. "If we try to go any farther somebody'll chop us off at the knees."

He tested the door and found it open, the shack deserted. "Stay outside and keep your eyes peeled," he said. Finding a kerosene lamp, he spread kerosene on the floor and up the walls. He saved some and spilled it in a line out into the dry grass, as far as it would go. Then he fished in his pocket for the matches. "The boys ain't going to appreciate this much, so get ready to run."

He pulled up a handful of dry grass, twisted it, then used his body to shield it from the breeze until the match's tiny flame took hold and the grass blazed up. He dropped it into the heavy grass around the cowshed. In moments the flames were racing through the grass, found the kerosene, followed it across the clearing and up into the shack.

"It's pretty," Dundee said, "but let's don't wait for the whole show." They struck out in a hard run for the clump of liveoaks. A shout went up, and another and another. Dogs barked. In a moment men were running in the street, hollering, everybody trying to give orders. A few wild shots were fired. Dundee mounted the bay. "Let's go back up on the hill where the view is better."

They were halfway there when Tobe Crane said, "Dundee, you notice something?"

"What?"

"The breeze has stopped."

Dundee reined up and looked back. He saw the shack collapse in a shower of sparks, the flames leaping high, then dying down. But Tobe was right. The breeze had quit. There was nothing to carry the flames any farther up the street.

"One cowshed and one flea-ridden shack," Dundee gritted. "But at least we got our exercise."

Dundee got more exercise that night, pacing, worrying, thinking about Hardesty's outside men coming to stop the siege, and maybe laying out a bunch of well-intentioned cowboys in the grass to stay. By daylight he was up, sleepy-eyed and irritable. He hadn't slept much. He went down and pulled four men out of the line and put them off on horseback to patrol as outriders, to watch for anyone who might be coming to give aid to the town. One by one he gave the message to the other men: "If trouble comes, the signal will be three shots, fired as quick as a man can pull the trigger. You get on your horse and get there as fast as you can ride. Scattered, we may not put up much fight. Together, we'll give them their money's worth."

Later Dundee sipped coffee and watched John Titus through narrowed eyes. *Crazy old man. Wants revenge worse than he wants to stop the cattle thieving. He could've cleaned this country up, hitting a camp at a time. But he's got to take on the whole town. Crazy old man.*

The mood passed, for Dundee thought he could understand John Titus. Once, the cattle had been important. But that had been while he still had a son.

Dundee turned his attention to Tobe Crane. He thought of Millie McCown. The last thing in his mind as he dozed off to sleep was a mental picture of Tobe holding Millie's hand as they all stood at Son Titus' grave.

Three quick-paced shots brought him out of the nap and onto his feet, grabbing at his carbine. He blinked away the sleep and saw one of the Titus cowboys spurring toward him on the trail that led in from the northeast. The cowboy shouted, "They're coming! They're coming!"

He slid his horse to a stop. Dundee glanced down the hill and saw the scattered Titus cowboys beginning to get into their saddles. It would take a while before they could all get here.

"Who's coming?" he demanded.

"I don't know," the rider blurted, face flushed with excitement. "I didn't let them get close enough to tell. But Dundee . . . Mister Titus . . . there's a hell of a bunch of them. Must be forty . . . maybe fifty."

Dundee swallowed, his fists going tight. This was what he had been afraid of. He glanced back down the hill again, mentally calculating how long it would take all the Titus cowboys to get here.

"How much time we got?"

"They're right on us."

Dundee could see the dust now, and he knew the cowboys wouldn't get here in time, not enough of them. At this moment there were only five: himself, John Titus, Tobe, the outrider and a man who had stayed at the chuckwagon to cook. "Let's get to cover," he shouted. "Maybe we can give them something to chew on till the rest of the boys reach here."

He threw himself down behind a heavy liveoak, the saddlegun ready. Old John Titus knelt behind another, rifle resting against the trunk. Tobe Crane lay on his belly, favoring the wounded arm, holding a pistol in his hand.

Dundee took a deep breath, then drew a bead on the lead rider. He would wait until he knew he couldn't miss.

John Titus shouted. Dundee tried not to be distracted, but he lost his head. The old man shouted again. "It's *our* bunch, Dundee! It's ours!"

Dundee lowered the carbine. "What'd you say?"

"It's my neighbors, Dundee, the ones I sent for. That's old Charlie Moore there in the lead. I'd know his dun horse anywhere. And that man on the *grulla*, he's Walter Matthews of the Half Circle M. They've come to help us."

Dundee pushed to his feet and took off his hat, wiping cold sweat from his forehead onto his sleeve.

In town, a commotion began in the streets as the new riders showed on the hill. Horses stirred dust. Men ran to and fro. Though the sound didn't carry, there was visible sign of violent argument. Some of the Titus cowboys started dropping slugs down there, adding to the melee. Then there came the muffled rumble of hoofs, the sharp shouts of excited men. Twenty or more horsemen spurred toward the south end of town, toward the river and the span of open country that stretched beyond.

"They're trying a break!" Dundee shouted. "Let's get them!"

He swung onto the bay and took the lead, moving headlong down the hill, angling southwestward, running over brush, scattering rocks. He didn't look back, but he could hear other horses running behind him. Dundee took an oblique course that he hoped would intercept the fleeing outlaws. He could see desperation in the way they spurred, flaying horses with their quirts. Some began snapping wild shots toward the Titus posse. None struck Dundee, and he didn't have time right now to see if they hit anyone else. he just kept spurring.

Now he could begin to make out faces. He looked for the bulky shape of Roan Hardesty but couldn't pick him out from the crowd. It occurred to him that the dappled gray wasn't in the bunch. Roan was still in town.

They've run out on him, he realized. *They seen they was whipped and then run out on him.*

He saw one face he knew too well. Jason Karnes, on the stocking-legged black. Dundee couldn't hear the words, but he could almost read them on the twisting lips of the black-whiskered outlaw. Karnes raised a six-shooter and snapped a shot at Dundee. His horse almost stumbled, and Karnes was busy a few seconds getting his balance. Then the pistol came up again.

Dundee swung his saddlegun into line. It was hard enough, making a shot from a running horse. It was almost impossible, making one to the right. Dundee tried to compensate by twisting his body as far as he could. He squeezed the trigger and knew he had missed. Karnes pulled closer, within pistol range. The pistol cracked again, and Dundee felt a tug at his sleeve, a searing pain as the bullet raked him.

Now the range was almost point blank. Dundee squeezed the trigger again. Karnes jerked backward, slipped over the horse's right hip and tumbled to the ground. Dundee lost sight of him in the dust as horses went over and past him.

Other shots were being fired. He saw the outlaws begin reining to a stop, trying to raise their hands. Some still spurred, attempting to outrun the cowboys.

Dundee's bay was slowing, tiring. Dundee let him bring himself slowly to a stop, for he knew the horse had about done its do. Around him, possemen were gathering in those fugitives who had quit. Others kept up the run.

They'll catch the most of them, he told himself. *I better get down yonder and see about Roan.*

Moving back toward town in a slow trot, he passed the still form of Jason Karnes. One look was enough. He took no pleasure in the sight, no satisfaction from bringing the outlaw down.

That's two I've took out of the family, he thought. *It ain't a thing to make a man proud.*

John Titus angled down to meet him, trailed by Tobe Crane. The old man knew before Dundee told him. "Roan's still in town."

Dundee nodded. "He wasn't with that bunch. They deserted him. Not many of them will get away."

Titus said severely: "I don't care so much about them. I want Roan."

"I'll go down there and see if I can find him."

"Roan's mine. I'm going with you."

Dundee wanted to argue, but he knew it would be useless. He glanced at the young cowboy. "You coming, Tobe?" When the cowboy answered yes, Dundee said: "Keep a sharp eye out, then. A cornered bear is apt to bite."

They rode slowly up the street, three abreast. Dundee's

sweeping gaze probed the open doors, the windows, the alleyways.

Titus called: "Roan! Roan, you come on out here. I want you."

No reply.

Ahead of them lay the Llano River Saloon. Instinctively Dundee felt drawn toward it. He'd seen Roan there before. He pointed and said quietly, "Mister Titus, I think yonder's the place."

He rode as close as he dared, then started to swing out of the saddle. Halfway down, he caught a glimpse of movement, saw the big man step out through the open doors, shotgun in his huge hands.

"Hold it right where you're at, Dundee! Don't move another inch."

Dundee halted, half in and half out of the saddle, the saddlegun in his right hand but not where he could swing it into play. Tobe Crane held a six-shooter uncertainly. John Titus just sat there staring down into the awesome bore of that shotgun, both hands resting easily on the saddlehorn. If he felt any fear, his face did not betray it.

Roan said in a heavy voice that was the mixture of anger and desperation: "John, I told you not to come down here. I told you I didn't kill that boy."

Titus was steady as an ancient liveoak. "If you're figuring on pulling that trigger, Roan, do it now. It's going to be you or me."

"John, we was friends once. I don't want to have to kill you."

"I come to hang you, Roan. I'll do it, unless you shoot me."

It came to Dundee with the force of a mule-kick what John Titus was attempting to do. He was trying to force Roan into shooting him, knowing Roan wouldn't live to get ten steps down the street. He was willing to throw himself away to see Roan Hardesty brought to the ground. "Mister Titus. . . ."

Titus ignored Dundee. He said: "Go on, Roan. Do it if you're going to. I'm fixing to draw my gun." The old man's hand slowly went down to his hip, closed over the pistol there and came up again. It seemed it took him all day.

Roan Hardesty's face whitened, and the blue blotches seemed to go almost black. For a moment it was in his eyes to pull the trigger. But then his chin fell. Slowly he let the muzzle of the shotgun sink toward the ground. He leaned on a tiepost for strength.

"I couldn't do it, John."

Titus said, "Get him, Dundee."

Dundee hesitated. "What you going to do?"

"Just what I said I was. I'm going to hang him."

"You can't do that. You got to wait for the Rangers."

"My boy'll sleep easy tonight. The man responsible for killing him will be dead."

"Mister Titus. . . ."

"Your work is finished, Dundee. I'm taking over now. We'll wait till the men get back. Then we'll take Roan to a fit place out yonder on the river. Runaway is fixing to die. We'll let him die with it."

Dundee glanced sadly at the aging outlaw, his eyes trying to tell Roan he was sorry now that he hadn't gotten away. Roan seemed to understand. "Don't worry yourself, Dundee. I already lived beyond my time. I wouldn't lie to you; I don't want to die. But I reckon I've had my day."

Dundee walked into the saloon, sick at heart. He rummaged around behind the bar and came up with part of a bottle of whisky. He stood in the door, leaning his shoulder against the jamb, drinking straight out of the bottle and watching the cowboys slowly drift in, bringing their prisoners with them—one here, two there, three in another bunch. Roan Hardesty sat slumped in a chair that had been dragged out into the street, the cowboys ringed around him. John Titus still sat on his horse, his leathery old face dark and grim.

A buckboard came down the street. Leaning out the door, Dundee saw Katy Long, a thin girl riding beside her. The girl was Lutie. The cowboys turned to stare. Katy pulled her team to a halt and took a long, apprehensive look at Roan Hardesty. Then her eyes went to Dundee. She jumped down from the buckboard and motioned for Lutie to follow. The girl moved slowly, reluctantly. Katy rushed to Dundee's side.

"What're they going to do to Roan?"

"John Titus says he's fixing to hang him."

"He can't."

"With all them cowboys? He can do anything he damn pleases."

"It's not right, Dundee. Roan didn't kill Son Titus."

"You know it, and I know it. I think even John Titus knows it. But we can't prove which one of his men did do it, so Roan pays."

Katy's eyes turned blue with regret. "Dundee, I've got something to tell you. I didn't want to, didn't intend to. But now it's the only way. It's got to be done."

"Tell me what?"

"I'll let Lutie." She motioned for the girl. Lutie came to her unwillingly, dragging her feet, looking at the floor. "Lutie, you tell Dundee what you told me."

When Lutie's story was over, Dundee found his left fist clenched so tightly the knuckles were white. He lifted the bottle and took a long, long swallow. He cut his eyes to the girl and demanded threateningly, "You sure you ain't lying to me?"

Frightened, Lutie shook her head. Katy said protectively: "She's telling the truth, Dundee. Added to everything else, it figures."

Dundee turned and hurled the bottle at the saloon wall. It shattered, the whisky spattering and running down to the floor. He rubbed his hand across his face, then stalked out into the street. He strode to where John Titus sat on his horse.

"Mister Titus, you've trusted me for weeks now. Do you still trust me?"

Surprised, the old ranchman said, "Sure, Dundee."

"Then trust me when I tell you old Blue Roan didn't kill your boy. It wasn't Roan, and it wasn't none of Roan's men."

"Then who was it?"

"I can't tell you yet. I know, but it's something I got to handle myself. Trust me."

"Dundee, I got to have more to go on than this. I got to. . . ."

"You got to wait. You got to let Roan live till I get back. Then you'll know the whole thing. Will you do that? Will you trust me?"

The old man stammered. "I ought not to . . . but I will, Dundee. I'll wait."

Dundee turned. "Katy, if I ain't back in a reasonable time, you tell John Titus what you told me."

Katy's voice held a tremor. "Dundee, you better take some help with you."

He shook his head. "This job I got to handle alone." He mounted the bay and rode toward the hill.

XIV

Ahead of him lay the creek, and beyond that the McCown headquarters. Face rigid, his jaw set square, Dundee rode toward the spring where Uncle Ollie McCown sat watching him. Ollie had his fishing pole, the hook sunk into the water below the spring.

"Howdy, Dundee," he called. "You-all do up your business in Runaway?"

Dundee stared hard at the old man, wondering how much he knew. "Ollie, I'm looking for Warren."

The tone of his voice betrayed him, for Ollie shrank back. Dundee could see realization sinking in. "Ollie, I asked you, where's Warren at?"

Ollie's voice was strained. "Big bunch of men rode by here some hours ago, on their way to help you-all. I reckon you took good care of old Roan and his bunch by now, didn't you?"

Now Dundee was convinced: Ollie knew. He might not have participated, but he knew.

"Ollie, I know the whole thing now. I'll ask you one more time, where's Warren?"

Ollie looked down at the water. "Dundee, Millie's up at the house. I bet she'll be real tickled to see you back. She baked up some cookies. They'd sure go good with a cup of coffee. I bet you and her could find a right smart to talk about." He paused, trying to gather strength. "She thinks the world of you, Dundee. If you was to ask her, she'd marry you in a minute. You could do a lot worse. She's a good girl."

"Ollie, does she know anything about this?"

Quickly the old man blurted: "She don't know nothing, Dundee. Warren didn't tell her nothing, and he'd of beat me to death if I'd ever even hinted to her. . . ." He realized he had said too much. He looked down at the fishing line again. Cold sweat broke on his forehead.

Dundee said, "Ollie, I still want to know . . ."

The old man wiped his sleeve over his face. "Sure is hot." His voice was almost gone. He was on the verge of crying. "Seems like it gets hotter every year. Things ain't what they used to be. Things has gone to hell, seems like. Time was when the world was fresh and sweet as dew. Now everything's got a bitter taste, and there's no pleasure left in being alive. It's hell to be an old man, Dundee."

Pitying him, Dundee turned away.

He rode to the house. Millie came out into the doorway, trying to brush back her long hair with her hand. She smiled, and her face was so pretty Dundee could feel his heart tearing in two. The joy that danced in her brought the bite of tears to his own.

"Dundee, is it all over with? Are you all right?"

He clenched his teeth and tried not to look at her. He couldn't help it; he had to look, and he felt his throat tighten. "Millie, I've got to see Warren. Is he here?"

She caught the gravity in his eyes now, and in his voice. Her joy faded, and worry rushed in. "He's up yonder working on his rock corrals. What's the matter, Dundee?''

He looked toward the rock pens that were the symbol of a man's driving ambition, of a poverty-born obsession for acquiring land and cattle, for building a protective wall of stolen wealth around him so that never again could he slide back into the squalor that had scarred his soul.

Millie demanded: "There's something wrong, Dundee. What is it?''

"I'll have to let Warren tell you."

He pulled away from her and rode toward the pens. He didn't dare look back, but he knew she was standing there watching him, confusion and fear crowding in around her. Though she did not know it yet, her world was about to come tumbling down; her anchor of security was about to be dragged away.

Warren McCown stood behind a half-finished rock fence sweat soaking his dirt-crusted shirt, rolling down his sun-browned face. Dundee guessed that by his own appearance and manner he was betraying himself, for he could see suspicion in Warren McCown.

"What's the trouble, Dundee?''

"Maybe you ought to tell *me*, Warren. Maybe you ought to tell me what really happened to Son Titus.''

Warren tensed. They stared at each other a long time in silence. "You know as much as I do, Dundee.''

"Maybe, I think I've figured out some things now. For one thing, I know why you used to have trouble with Roan Hardesty and his men. It wasn't for the reason you said, that they was driving stolen cattle across your land. It was because you was in competition with them. Old Roan wanted to run things in this country, but you was stealing for yourself and wouldn't split anything with him.

"That time you went south to buy cattle . . . you went north first. You stole T Bar cattle from old Titus, drove them south and traded them for cattle that had been stole down on the border. That way you didn't have any T Bar stuff on your country.''

"You got an awful imagination, Dundee.''

"Not very. That cowboy that helped you . . . first thing he done when he left here was to head for Runaway to fill his belly full of liquor and wrap himself around a soft, warm town girl. He told her things he ought to've kept to himself. Then Son Titus came along, and he found that girl. He got her drunk enough that she told him things *she* ought to've kept quiet. Last time he left Runaway he was coming out here to brace you with the facts. Somewhere out yonder you ran into each other, and you killed him.''

Warren McCown rubbed his sweaty hands on the legs of his britches. ''What you figure on doing, Dundee?''

''I figure on taking you to the Rangers. If old John Titus gets hold of you, he'll hang you.''

Warren's face twisted in bitterness. ''Titus. It's always been a Titus. I told you my daddy died on a ranch, didn't I, Dundee? But I didn't tell you which one. It was the Titus ranch. Daddy had dragged us there just the week before, the way he dragged us everywhere, hungry and broke and wearing castoff clothes that nobody else wanted. Old man John Titus was so big he didn't know the names of half his men. I doubt he ever even seen my daddy. Son Titus was just a button then but spoiled rotten as a barrelful of bad apples. He was playing around the herd instead of tending to his job, and he let a big steer get out. Daddy spurred off after him, and his horse fell. Daddy never knew what hit him. They buried him right there on the Titus ranch, gave us kids a couple of months' wages and told us how bad they felt. Well, John Titus has owed us something for that, something a lot more than a little handful of money.''

''He didn't owe you his boy's life.''

''I didn't want to kill him. He forced it on me. Said he'd take away everything we had and burn our place to the ground. I'd put in too many years of sweat. I couldn't let him wreck us.''

''I got to take you in, Warren. Maybe a jury will see your side and go easy.''

''And what happens to Millie? What happens to this place? No, Dundee. You're not taking me anywhere.''

Dundee reached for his pistol. Warren moved suddenly, crouching behind the rock fence and coming up with a rifle.

Dundee shouted: "Don't be a fool, Warren. Kill me and there'll be others. There'll be no end to it."

But he saw the intention in Warren's eyes as the rifle came up into line. Dundee threw himself off the bay as the first shot exploded. He went down on his hands and knees. For a couple of seconds he was shielded by the frightened horse. He used that time to get moving toward another section of rock fence. He vaulted over and dropped behind it as the rifle cracked again.

At the house he heard Millie screaming. He glanced in that direction and saw Uncle Ollie hobbling up as fast as he could from the spring. Millie ran toward the corral, crying: "Warren! Dundee!"

Dundee raised up enough to see over the fence. He leveled the pistol where he thought Warren would come up. He saw the top of Warren's head, then the rifle. Warren arose, drawing a bead. This time, Dundee knew with a sickening certainty, Warren wasn't going to miss. Not if Dundee let him fire.

Dundee squeezed the trigger. He saw Warren lurch back, heard the rifle clatter against the stone. He jumped up and ran around the fence. Under the breath he was praying.

He stopped abruptly, his blood cold. He turned, then Millie came running, crying. "Warren! What did you do to Warren?"

Dundee grabbed her. "Millie, don't go back there!"

She beat at him with her fists. Hysterically she screamed: "Let me go! Let me go!" She twisted away from him and ran on. At the fence she stopped, her voice lifting in agony.

The bay had tangled in the reins a little way down toward the house. Walking in that direction, Dundee met the struggling Ollie McCown. The old man looked at him, his eyes begging. "God, Dundee, how am I going to tell her?"

Dundee shook his head, his eyes afire so that he could barely see. "I don't know, Ollie. I don't know if you ever can."

The ride to town was one of the longest Dundee had ever made, seemed like. It was full dark long before he got there. He found the cowboys scattered in the buildings up and down the long, crooked street. The Rangers had arrived to take charge and collect any prisoners on whom they had claims. Katy Long was back in her saloon, serving liquor to John Titus.

The old man looked up as Dundee walked through the door into the lamplight. His eyes seemed to have softened now. Maybe it was Katy's whisky.

"Dundee, where's McCown?"

Tightly Dundee said, "He's dead."

The old man nodded gravely. "This girl here, she told me the whole thing, once you was a long ways down the road. I reckon it was tough on you."

"Life's always been tough on me."

John Titus pushed the bottle at Dundee. Dundee took it, though he absently rolled it in his hands instead of drinking from it. "Where's Tobe Crane?"

Somebody went out and fetched the cowboy. Dundee looked up painfully. "Tobe, Warren McCown is dead. I killed him." He took a long drink then, and followed it with another. "Millie's the one who'll suffer the most. She needs somebody right now. I think she needs *you*."

The cowboy just stood and stared at him.

Impatiently Dundee demanded: "You love her, don't you? You as much as told me so."

"I love her, Dundee."

"Then go to her. She'll never need you more than she needs you now."

Tobe turned to go. Dundee said: "And Tobe . . . you be real good to that girl, you hear me?"

"I will."

Dundee turned back to the bottle. He didn't quit drinking till his head was starting to spin. It occurred to him suddenly that he hadn't seen Roan Hardesty. He half-shouted: "Where's Roan? John Titus, you promised me. . . ."

Titus shook his head. "Don't worry. Roan has took to the tulies." He pointed his stubbled chin toward Katy

Long. "After this girl here told me what she did, I got to thinking. When the Rangers got here, they'd take old Roan and lock him up, and he'd never see sunlight again the rest of his days. He's an old man, Roan is. He ain't got many years left."

"You mean you just let him go?"

"We was friends once. *He* remembered it. He couldn't bring himself to shoot me. After I found out the truth of what happened to Son, I couldn't bring myself to see him rot away in a cell the few years he's got left. So I told him to head south for Mexico."

"He's liable to take some of your cattle with him as he goes."

Titus looked surprised, as if that thought hadn't occurred to him. Then he shrugged. "You can't expect an old man to go hungry."

Next morning the Rangers had picked out the men they intended to take to jail. The rest of the prisoners were turned loose and advised to see how far they could get without stopping to rest their horses.

Titus' foreman, Strother James, looked down the emptying street. "It'll be a funny-looking town, nobody living in it."

Titus said: "It won't be no town atall. We're going to burn it."

"All of it?"

"Every stick. Get the men started at the job."

They began at the far end, setting the buildings afire one at a time. Some had rock walls that wouldn't burn, but the roofs would go, and the floors if they had any.

Dundee said: "Mister Titus, I got money coming. I'd like to collect it now and be on my way."

Disappointed, Titus said: "We need you here, Dundee. I was hoping you'd stay."

Dundee shook his head. "I studied on it awhile, but I'm afraid this part of the country is spoiled for me now. It's best I go on."

"Any idea where?"

"West someplace. Don't make much difference."

"I ain't got much cash with me. I'll give you all I got

and send the rest on to a bank where you can pick it up. How about Pecos City?"

Dundee shrugged. "Pecos City would be all right. I expect it's a good place to get drunk."

Katy Long had her team hitched to the buckboard and was carrying out what belongings she could pack into it. A couple of cowboys were helping her load a trunk. Dundee looked down the street where the plumes of smoke were rising. They'd be to the Llano River Saloon in a few minutes now, sprinkling kerosene, striking matches.

Dundee said, "Too bad about your place here."

She didn't appear upset. "It's worn itself out anyhow. There are other places down the road, fresh places."

"Got any particular one in mind?"

"Nope. Thought I might ride along with you if it's all right. A woman alone . . . no telling what might happen."

He shook his head. "You can take care of yourself; I don't worry none about that. As for me, I got some problems to think out. It's better I ride by myself. *Adios,* Katy. Maybe I'll see you someplace."

He swung up onto his horse, nodded at John Titus and took the trail that led around the bluff and west from Runaway.

John Titus disconsolately watched him go. "Dundee's a good man. I hate to lose him."

Katy said, "*I* don't intend to lose him."

"I'm sending him some money. He's supposed to pick it up in Pecos City," Titus suggested. He looked at the girl, and his eyes came as near smiling as they had in a long time. "Whichaway you headed?"

She arched her wrist as invitation for one of the cowboys to help her into the buckboard. Half a dozen rushed to do it. Seated, she smiled back at the old ranchman.

"I've been thinking I'd try Pecos City."

She flipped the lines, and the team took her west, while the dark smoke that had been Runaway rose into the blue summer skies and slowly dissipated over the rocky Llano River hills.